Dead South

THE LOWCOUNTRY MYSTERY SERIES: BOOK ONE

David Banner

Chapter One

If Detective Ryan Devereux would have known a simple phone call was going to change his life forever, he probably would've thought twice before stepping off his houseboat. That's the thing about life-changing moments though. You almost never see them coming, and this one was miles away from what Ryan expected to find on his first week back with the Charleston County Police Department.

Having grown up in what was often referred to as the friendliest city in America, he was the definition of a true Southerner. Ryan grew up on sweet tea, Sunday mass, and more fried chicken than any one person had the right to eat. Unless, of course, that person happened to be raised by Melissa Devereux. Known as one of the best cooks in all of Charleston County, it wasn't long after having her babies that Melissa decided to open her own little café. Besides, it wasn't as though she had much else keeping her busy with her husband gone off to only God knows where to defend his country.

And wouldn't you just know it, Ryan was named an employee on the spot. It never seemed to bother his mother—or anyone else, for that matter—that the young boy could barely see over the counter. His sweet smile and bright blue eyes were enough to make almost all of Mrs. Devereux's patrons light up with joy every time they walked through the door. Yes, the fried chicken may have been cooked to perfection, but to the elderly church-going folks around Charleston, it was the soft smile of a little boy that made for a sweet ending to their meals.

The call came early in the morning, just as the bright orange sun began to rise out of the eerily still Atlantic waters. Since moving into his houseboat, *Second Wind*, he'd gotten accustomed to staying up a bit later than he was able to with a wife lying next to him. And now that that kind of thing was no longer a problem, he found himself enjoying more late evenings than he had any right to.

There was something so undeniably soothing about the crashing waves and the moonlight. With a cold drink in his hand and a few old memories on his mind, Ryan always managed to find himself lost in the idea of the ocean and the possibilities it seemed to hold.

"The property owner found her this morning," said a red-haired officer. He was new to the force, a rookie in every sense of the word, which meant he'd seen far less than the seasoned detective. A good thing, if you were to ask Ryan. So good that he might just tell the young cop to consider a different career path before becoming too jaded with the harsh reality of being in law enforcement.

He knew better, though. Being a police officer took a certain kind of person, one with the desire to make things right, to find the truth in the lies, and to hold the guilty accountable for their crimes. That kind of thing was just in a man's blood, period. Once he found it, there seemed to be no turning back, no denying it.

There was no crunch of leaves, no snapping of twigs underfoot, and no rustling of dry foliage in the breeze. The previous night's heavy spring thunderstorm had made sure of that. The detective's shiny black shoes sank into the soft marshland with every step, covering them in a thick, sloshy mess of leaves and mud. It was nothing new, though. Living in South Carolina's Lowcountry meant many things, and chief among them was the understanding that shoes weren't meant to stay shiny.

"Property owner?" the detective asked, following behind the young rookie.

The words struck his ears like church bells, loud and sudden if you weren't expecting them. Waverly Plantation hadn't been in use for the last ten years, ever since "Old Man Waverly" was found at the end of his driveway with a broken leg and the morning mail scattered around him like gossip at a cotillion.

Seeing as how his son was too busy chasing his dreams up in New York somewhere, Ronald Waverly had spent the last five years of his life being cared for in the local rest home. The idea of such a thing always rubbed Ryan the wrong way, leaving the man who raised you with strangers. In his eyes, it simply lacked proper respect.

"Yes," the young man replied. "The property was bought a few months ago by someone out of Valdosta, Georgia. A family, I think. The owner was out exploring the marsh when he spotted an old rusted-out boat and decided to check it out."

"I see," Ryan answered. "And where is the owner now?"

"I believe he's being questioned in the house. I don't believe we've met." The young man cleared his throat, then awkwardly extended his hand. "My name is Carter White."

"Good to meet you, Officer White." Ryan shook the young man's hand. "How long have you been on the force?"

"About a month now. I started in early June." There was a shaky hesitation in his voice, one the senior detective interpreted as nerves. Though honestly, he couldn't remember being so shy, even as a rookie.

"Well that explains it," Ryan said. "I was out for the beginning of the month."

"I hope everything is okay," he replied, dropping the octave of his voice just a little.

"Everything is fine," Ryan answered, not particularly wanting to get into the complicated story of his current situation. "Just needed to get a few things together."

"If there's anything I can do to help—"

"I appreciate it," Ryan interrupted. "I'll manage. Now where is the victim?"

Officer White pointed. "Just past this tree line."

Waverly Plantation was one of the largest properties in Charleston County. The land had seen many changes over its long history. Built as a rice farm, which any true Southerner would claim as one of South Carolina's most important antebellum crops, the land was home to a long line of Waverly men in the years that followed. A large white plantation house sat at the end of a long tree-lined driveway. In the back sat a series of small houses, once home to a number of slaves in its early stages. After the shameful defeat of the Civil War, however, Waverly Plantation had transformed into a produce farm.

There was still something thick in the air, something a little darker than the dense southern humidity. Like so many places, lives had begun and ended on that property. Each one was a different story in the rich tapestry of Charleston County, each one remembered by the people who, generations later, still walked the same land as their ancestors.

The sound of Detective Devereux's phone rang out through the swamp-covered land, ricocheting from the moss-covered trees before vanishing into the dark woods. Removing the device from his pocket, Ryan saw a familiar face fill the screen, one that caused him to feel a series of emotions, each one conflicting with the last.

"Be careful." Carter pointed. "I dropped my phone in a marsh last week. Instant water damage."

"It's okay," Ryan said, taking stock of the lithe-limbed man. "I live on a boat. My case is waterproof."

"That's Jillian Hathaway. I recognize her from the paper."

"Yes," Ryan replied, declining the call and sliding the phone back into his pocket.

Though the thought of speaking with her so early in the morning wasn't something he was crazy about, he would have still answered the woman if not for the fact that he was busy with the matter at hand. A woman had, in all likelihood, been murdered, and it was Ryan's job to find the truth of how she'd ended up alone and lifeless in a marsh.

Carter smiled. "She's engaged, I think. To that news guy. You know her?"

"I do," he answered, stepping out of the tree line and onto the banks of a small pond. "We used to be married."

Spanish moss hung in massive tendrils over a black body bag that lay just a few feet from the water. Even in his earliest childhood memories, Ryan found himself amazed by the mystery and ambience of the moss, the way it only grew near the hot southern shores, the way it called out to him, reminding him of home in a way few other things could.

"Thank you." Ryan turned to Carter. "I've got it from here."

Tipping his hat, the young man stepped back, making sure to distance himself before turning his back to his superior. It wasn't necessary, not at all. But that didn't mean the detective didn't appreciate the simple act of Southern respect.

"Sleeping in again?" Kit asked. "I've been here for fifteen minutes."

"What do we have?" he asked, batting away her thinly-veiled jab.

Kit Walker was a firecracker, though not in the way you'd expect. Both full of energy and completely calculated, she was like a quiet storm, just waiting offshore for an opportunity to strike. Arriving from New Jersey just over a year ago, she'd been partnered with Detective Devereux almost immediately. It seemed the police chief thought she could use a little Southern flavor in her diet, and who better to give her that than Ryan Devereux?

"Skeletal remains. Female. Likely late teens or early twenties," she answered flatly.

Ryan looked to his partner. "Is it one of ours?"

It had been almost two years since he'd been assigned to the cold-case department. And in that time, he'd handled mostly older, unsolved cases that often didn't even include a body. So finding himself among the first people called to investigate struck him as a little odd. In the beginning, Ryan found himself missing the usual detective work, but thanks to Charleston County's police chief, cold-case was more of a title than a cage. Many nights, Ryan found himself driving the winding backroads of Lowcountry doing what he'd always done as a detective. Serving justice.

"Can't be sure," Kit answered, kneeling down and unzipping the black bag. "Looks like she was headed to a wedding. She was certainly dressed for the occasion."

"What do you mean?" he asked.

"Look." Kit spread the bag. "It's a bridesmaid's dress."

It was an image he hadn't seen in years, one he'd tried to keep from creeping back into his mind on the days he drove down Market Street and past his old high school. But standing there, feeling the thick humidity lick his skin and the sound of gnats buzzing near his ear, there was no denying the truth. Ryan Devereux knew exactly who lay on the ground in front of him.

"It's not a bridesmaid's dress," he said, staring down at the dirty, tattered blue gown. He remembered the way her face looked that day in the store, the nervous smile on her lips as Ryan handed the cashier a one-hundred-dollar bill. They were so young then, so in love. At least, that's what he thought. He sighed. "It's a prom dress."

"How do you know?" Kit raised an eyebrow.

"Because I bought it for her."

Chapter Two

A quick look at his phone let Ryan know where to find Foggy King, brother of Haley King and the kid he'd always hated growing up. While it would take a little while for a positive identification to come in, the detective knew without question who the body in the marsh would turn out to be.

Foggy King was the proud owner of Kingfish, one of Charleston's most popular bars. Though looking at the place from the outside, you'd have never guessed it. Miles off the main thoroughfare but only a stone's throw from the ocean, the bar quickly became a favorite among local Charlestonians. While you'd mainly find fishermen, shrimpers, and often a few businessmen looking to blow off steam, every few weeks, a group of new adults would pop in, quickly decide the crowd was a little 'too old' for them, and head back out the door after a drink or two.

Ryan could only hope news of the man's sister hadn't made it to him yet, though with no positive ID, he doubted much gossip could spread about the find over at the Waverly Plantation. The evening sun was beginning its slow dive into the endless blue water, casting shadows over the small backroads leading to Kingfish. It was truly a beautiful sight, though he didn't really take time to look.

It seemed no matter which road he drove, which corner he turned, or which house he passed, Ryan Devereux managed to find memories along the way. What else is to be expected, though, when you've spent your entire life in a place? Especially one like Charleston County, with its endless array of beaches, swamps, and slow-talking Southerners.

The unmistakable sound of crushing gravel under his tires bellowed up from the soft country ground. It was still early enough that there were only a handful of cars in the parking lot, most of them pickup trucks or late-model, often rusted coupes. There was just something about the Lowcountry that made folks care a little less about the cars they drove.

Sure, in other places, a new car could be seen as a sign of something—money, success, and even privilege. But in Charleston, it just seemed like another thing to have to clean when it came time for thunderstorms with dirt roads. Besides, most folks around there probably weren't going too far anyway. After all, South Carolina Lowcountry was best seen by way of slow, easy strolls around town. Everyone knew that.

Stepping out on the gravel and slamming the door to his silver Chrysler, the detective thought about Haley King, about how much she'd once meant to him. He remembered the way his heart fluttered and skipped at the thought of asking her to prom and how excited he'd gotten when she said yes. He could even still hear her voice telling him everything would be okay after his momma died during his junior year.

There'd always been a wonderful sweetness to the girl, an easiness he'd once found so much comfort and joy in having by his side. It just seemed those days were over in a flash, coming to an end so suddenly. He'd spent a long while wondering if they'd even been real.

"Not often I see you." Foggy said, wiping down the bar in front of him. "Am I in some kind of trouble?"

Foggy was six foot two inches of pure Southern country boy, with sandy-brown hair, a tan that looked like he enjoyed the outdoors a little more than indoors, and a thick Carolina twang in his words. A grey Henley shirt wrapped his thick upper body and a silver crucifix hung from his neck as he stood behind the high wooden bar.

"I've been a little busy," the detective answered. "And no, you haven't broken any law. At least none I'm aware of."

Ever since the disappearance of Foggy's little sister twenty years ago, the men couldn't help but feel tied together in a way that most others wouldn't understand, though with their tumultuous relationship, they'd had little contact over the last few years. It was Foggy who'd first come to Ryan's house, insisting his sister had vanished after leaving for prom. Then in a move he'd spent years feeling guilty over, Ryan had sent the young man away.

It's hard, though, when you're young. Even the smallest heartbreak can feel like the biggest thing in the world. That was especially true for Ryan, a young man in love. When the girl he'd cared so much for canceled their date only hours before the big night, Ryan swore to himself he wouldn't call her again, he wouldn't look at her, and he wouldn't give her his tears. But like many times after, he was about as wrong as a sinner in church.

"How have you been?" Ryan asked.

"Well enough, I guess." Foggy slid an icy-cold Corona across the bar. "Finally got that old truck fixed up."

"The Chevy?"

"Yes." Foggy adjusted his navy baseball cap. "I was out front washing her down and a guy stopped by, made me an offer."

"You gonna sell?" Ryan asked, taking a sip.

"I'm thinking about it."

"Was the offer good?" he asked, placing the cold bottle back on the wooden bar, watching as cool beads of condensation rolled down the white and gold label.

"Oh, yeah. It was fine offer. He even offered more when I didn't agree right away. I just wasn't expecting it so fast. Tell me why you're here. What do you want?"

"To tell you something," Ryan replied, thinking back to the hot summer days of his childhood, remembering the hell Foggy's daddy raised after he stole that truck and smashed it into the guard rail off Route Seven.

"And what is that?"

"I wanted to talk to you about Haley."

Just as they had ever since the night his sister vanished, Foggy's eyes shifted at the mention of her name, though with each passing year, that shift moved a little slower, with a little more hesitation than it once had. But hope is a finite thing. It dwindles with each new dawn, stepping a little farther away from us.

"We don't have to keep hashing this out, man. Let's just remember her the way—"

"We found her," Ryan said, not looking up from his Corona. "This morning."

A quiet stillness fell across the air, turning the small space between the two men into a cavernous void of discomfort and painful memories. There'd been a time, very early on, when the mention of his sister's name would have inspired a sense of reserved hope in him, but now, twenty years later, the bartender had seen enough disappointment to know better.

"Where?" he asked, polishing a shot glass.

"The old Waverly Plantation," the detective replied. "We're still waiting on the official identification but . . . it's her."

"All these years," Foggy said, tears pooling in his eyes. "All these years, and she was just down the road. Doesn't seem right, does it?"

"None of this seems right," Ryan answered, turning away a little as the man flecked a tear from his cheek.

"What does this mean?" Foggy asked. "What happens next?"

"It means we need to figure out what happened to her. It's gonna be hard to tell anything from the remains. We're still waiting for the coroner."

"Remains," Foggy said, finally looking up. "God, that's what she is now, isn't it?"

"She was in the marsh, held under by an old rusted-out boat," Ryan said, making eye contact.

"That means we can finally put this thing to rest," he said after a long minute.

"Someone killed her, Foggy. We need to—"

"I can't deal with this right now," he said, waving Ryan off. "I just . . . business hasn't been great. I've got a lot on my plate."

"This is your sister," Ryan said.

"I know that," Foggy sneered. "And I don't mean to be rude, but she's *my* sister. I'll deal with this the way I see fit."

"I'm afraid that's not how this works, Foggy. This is my job," Ryan answered, knowing full well there would be nothing he could say to sway the man's feelings about reopening the case, about knowing for a fact that the only thing left of his sister was a skeleton in a prom dress. "I know we've talked about it. But its been a while and I need to ask again. Is there anything you remember, anything from that night or the days leading up to it?"

"Shut up," Foggy murmured. "It's been twenty years. Twenty years, and the police didn't do a damn thing." He grunted. "Get out!" he yelled, pouring himself a shot of Kentucky bourbon. "I've replayed those days a million times in my head, man. You know that. My mother begged the police to help and they did nothing. Now suddenly, you're gonna come along and make everything okay. Yeah, right!"

"It was a different time. They just assumed she was a runaway. That was the normal response back then." Ryan sighed. "I'm not trying to make it right. I'm just trying to finally solve this thing. You know she didn't go into that marsh willingly."

"I won't go through this again, Ryan," Foggy snarled. "I drove myself crazy for years. I watched this thing tear my family apart. I can't do it again."

There was a weakness in his voice, a reservation that let Ryan know everything he needed to about how Foggy was going to handle this. He was strong, sure. That came from years of South Carolina backroads and his Lowcountry roots. But that strength rested on a cornerstone of fragile compartmentalization, one he'd spent the last twenty years building.

"What about the house?" Ryan asked. "I know you inherited it a couple of years back. You still own it, right?"

"Don't even think about it," he snapped. "Her room is still just as she left it. My mom made sure of that. It was the only small thing she could do. I won't let you tear through it like a bloodhound."

"I need to see that room."

"You need to drop this before you make me do something I'll regret."

"I can get a search warrant," Ryan replied. "If I need to."

"Why is everyone in this damn town so intent on destroying what's left of us?" Foggy ended the conversation, scooping up the empty Corona bottle and tossing it in the trash.

There was something terribly unique about the South's blistering summer heat. It seemed to hold a truth deep within its stiff and muggy presence. Detective Devereux headed back to the parking lot through the curtains of Spanish moss that seemed to grow thicker and denser with each summer day. Long ago, before divorce, crime, and the troubles of adulthood, there was a thought in his mind that maybe one day, he'd learn to hide behind that moss, to use it as camouflage in a world he wanted so desperately to find the truth in.

Unbuttoning the neck of his shirt and loosening his tie, Ryan paused for a minute in the cool shade, trying his best to let some of the built-up humidity escape his crisp cotton shirt. There were times when he'd considered wearing something less traditional to work, but somehow, the thought of showing up in flip-flops and board shorts didn't seem too professional. Not that it mattered in that moment. He was headed back to *Second Wind* where he would shower and get ready for dinner with his daughter.

Chapter Three

Detective work always seemed to come naturally to Ryan Devereux. There was a natural curiosity in his step, one he attributed to long, hot days behind the register of his mother's small café. People watching was a skill he'd developed at a young age, once he'd realized that hats weren't the only things left on the tables of a southern diner.

People liked to hide behind falsehoods and lies they hoped so desperately appeared true. They'd walk down the shady streets trying their best to hide in plain sight, hoping against hope that no one ever noticed the veiled truth in their steps. But there was always one thing that forced people to drop their pretenses and to step out into the sun. Give a man a fork, a knife, and a plate of piping-hot fried chicken, and well . . . all you have to do is sit back and watch the truth spread across that table like melted butter.

From almost the moment she could talk, the detective found that same thing to be true in his young daughter. Carly Devereux came as an unexpected surprise to Ryan and Jillian. The two were young, just out of school, with big dreams in their minds and not much money in their pockets. It was hard at first, and the stress of raising a child threatened to tear the young couple apart more than a few times. But the love of a man for his daughter is a strong thing, and every time Ryan got near that door, he paused just long enough to turn back and look into her bright blue eyes.

But there comes a time in every life when you just have to look in the mirror and find the hard truth. So as time marched by and the temperature began to rise, Ryan and Jillian finally decided to do what was best for the child they'd brought into this world.

"I spoke to your teacher yesterday," Ryan said, removing the cellphone from his daughter's hand and placing it on the far end of the table.

"They started it!" she snapped back.

"Hey." Ryan looked into her bright eyes. He'd always gone a little soft on the girl, preferring to let Jillian take the more authoritative role in dealing with her. Though over the last few years, he'd managed to teach her a few things too. He'd even managed to ground her a few times. "Don't snap at me. I'm just talking to you."

"Yes, sir," she replied, lowering her voice. "I'm not lying though. They started it. It was that stupid Danica Rosewood and her cheerleader friends. They said—"

"It doesn't matter what they said." Ryan placed his hand over his daughter's. Her soft features and small frame seemed to be changing by the day. He couldn't help but feel that each time he saw his child, she'd grown like Carolina Kudzu in the summer. "You can't stoop to that level. If you're gonna survive in this world, Carly, then you have to be strong. You have to let people's words just roll off your back. I've told you this."

"It just gets hard sometimes."

"I know. It can be hard for me too. But you just have to be strong. Don't react and don't run. Just stand your ground. If you do that, they'll back away."

"You ran," she responded, turning her gaze to a large picture window on the far side of the room. "You didn't stand your ground."

Marriage is a difficult thing. Anyone who's ever walked down an aisle could tell you that. But divorce was a whole other ballgame. You can love a child more than you ever thought you could. You can watch them grow and teach them everything you think they'll need to make it in this world. But sometimes, no matter how much they mean to you and how much you love them, you just can't stay. At least, not in the same house.

"We did what we thought was right," he answered. "For us, and for you. You're ten years old now. You're mature enough to understand. I know you are."

"I didn't say I didn't understand." She looked back at him. "But that doesn't mean I have to like it."

"I don't like it either."

It was true. From the moment he slid that ring on Jillian's finger, he never expected she'd one day be sliding it right back off and placing it in his hand. But love is a strange and powerful thing. Sometimes, that power isn't enough to drown out the world and the jagged, harsh truth it delivers with each coastal sunrise.

"He's loud, you know." Carly looked to her father, giving a coy smile. "And he thinks he's this really great cook, but the food is just weird. I don't like it."

The thought of another man raising his child was one that had always rubbed Ryan the wrong way. Especially one as self-absorbed as Thomas Kent, one of Charleston's better-known news anchors. But even with as much as he disliked the idea, the detective was always careful not to show his true feelings to the young girl.

"I'm sure it's not that bad."

"He made cream cheese grits, Dad," she said, extending her hands widely. "Cream. Cheese. Grits."

"That sounds . . ."

"Awful?" She smiled wide. "It was!"

"What about your mom?" Ryan asked before realizing the words had left his lips.

"She's . . . whatever." She waved her hand. "Same old Mom."

"Hopefully, that's a good thing."

"It is."

Opening the menu and scanning the selection, Ryan couldn't help but feel a little betrayed by his surroundings. There he sat, in the same building that had once housed his mother's small café, a place famous for fried chicken, meatloaf, and more fresh vegetables than you could shake a stick at. Gone were his mother's recipes, now replaced by things like the *'Screaming Elvis Burger'* and a *'Sweet Lotus Milkshake'*. Granted, he had no idea what either of those two things were, but he'd promised Carly the restaurant of her choice and he wanted to keep his word, even if it meant choking down something called *'Ring Of Fire Pasta'*.

"What are you doing this weekend?" he said through a mouthful of over-seasoned rigatoni.

"I'm not sure. Probably just hang out with Leah. Why?"

"I was going to ask if you wanted to see a movie or go to the beach."

"Sure." She smiled, taking a big gulp of her bright purple milkshake. "Can Leah come too?"

"I don't see why not. How about you just think about what you want to do and let me know?"

She smiled. "Cool."

Seeing another man's car parked in what was once his driveway still felt a little odd to the detective. Especially one as oversized and ostentatious as the shimmering red Audi Thomas Kent used to chauffeur his ex-wife and daughter around Charleston's famous historic district. Maybe it's true what they say about men and big cars. Maybe the guy was just trying to compensate for something. At least, that's what Ryan chose to believe.

"Okay." Ryan kissed his daughter's forehead as she stepped out onto the concrete driveway. "See you soon. I love you."

"Love you too." She smiled, then headed toward her waiting mother.

Jillian Hathaway, soon to be Jillian Kent, stood atop a large set of brick steps leading to her front door. Together, the two former partners had managed to scrape together enough money to afford them a small piece of Charleston's history. And for a while, it was the perfect home, filled with laughter, love, and wine. But as it tends to do, life came knocking and it was the young couple's turn to pay their debts.

It had been just over three years since the dissolution of his marriage to the beautiful Southern girl, and in that time, they'd managed to strike a balance. It wasn't easy in the beginning, but with each day, each Sunday dinner, and his daughter's sweet laughter, it became a little closer to normal. Ryan gave his ex-wife a smile, then left the driveway.

Chapter Four

It was almost ten o'clock when Ryan crossed the Stono River into Johns Island, South Carolina. Both the largest island in the state of South Carolina and Haley Kings's childhood home, the detective had spent much of his youth among the massive oak trees and sweeping ocean views. There'd always been a fondness in his heart for this and the many other barrier islands of the Lowcountry, though lately, he hadn't taken as much time to visit them as he'd have liked.

Old money created the lifeblood of Johns Island, showcased in large stately mansions lining the Atlantic coast. Each one was surrounded by trees planted generations before, with branches so thick and twisted they often left tourists in awe. It was that Old-South money that gave the King family such an easy life on the beautiful island.

Shifting his car into park and stepping out onto the concrete driveway, Ryan caught sight of the bright yellow moon reflecting against the waves. Sure, the sight of a moon's reflection on the waves could be seen in many places, but there was something wholly different about the way it looked from Charleston County. Some of the locals may even tell you it was a different moon altogether.

"Hey, man," Foggy said, opening the door.

"Hey," Ryan answered, stepping into the large beach house.

It was among the oldest on the island, though the King family made sure to always keep it updated and fresh. Its high ceilings and hardwood floors gave the perfect impression of easy coastal living and good taste. Foggy had his mother to thank for that. From almost the moment he was born into this world, Foggy's spoils were as thick as Carolina cotton, and just as plentiful too. His family's money could be traced back at least four generations to a wise young man with a shrewd mind for business and a talent for catching fish.

With little more than a fishing net and big conversation, Hobart King rose in status from the son of a homeless immigrant to the owner of one of Charleston's largest fisheries. And now, all these years later, it was Foggy who reaped the benefits of Hobart's good fortune. But it's like they say in the South, "Ain't nothing as real as the rain." And with a storm brewing just off the shore, the truth of what happened to his sister was about to come flowing across the South Carolina sand.

"Beer?" Foggy asked.

"Sure," Ryan replied, following him to the kitchen.

Both taller and thicker than the detective, Foggy King was often an intimidating sight for some, though Ryan knew him well enough to know no real danger lay under that imposing exterior. He still remembered the whispers around town all those years ago, the ones accusing the older brother of an involvement in his young sister's vanishing. But just as he had then, Ryan knew that simply wasn't the case. Yes, they'd had their spats from time to time, but what siblings didn't?

"It's all over the news," Foggy said, taking a seat on the large navy sofa.

His words were slow and his tone a little lower than it usually was. But who could blame him? That sort of news would upset even the strongest of men. So much time had passed since that night, so many lives changed, and chief among them were the lives of Haley's and Foggy's parents. Four years had passed since that night on the bridge, the night that had ended their father's life.

There'd been much loss in Foggy King's life, a world's worth of sorrow and heartbreak which could almost be felt emanating from the man at times. He was strong, though, rarely showing it to anyone else. Maybe it was tragedy or maybe it was the Lowcountry, but something connected the two men in a way they couldn't shake and never needed to discuss.

"I got the call earlier." Ryan sighed. "They checked it against her dental records. It's her."

"Yeah." Foggy sighed, running a hand through his shaggy brown hair. "I heard."

A thick southern breeze blew through the house from the open windows, gliding across the detective's skin like memories from long ago. He could almost hear Haley's laugh echoing through the halls as he thought back on those younger days. She'd been so happy, so vibrant and full of life, and suddenly, she was gone.

"I'm going to figure this out," the detective said, leaning forward in his oversized chair.

"How?" Foggy asked. "There's nothing but bones. It's been twenty years."

"That's my job. That's what I do."

"Maybe it would be easier to just let it go. Maybe we should just let her memory rest."

He'd seen it before, the pain that washed over someone when they spoke of someone they loved, someone the world had ripped away from them without a moment's notice. It was a hard thing to process, but it was especially hard for those involved in cold cases. No one wants to relive painful memories again. No one wants to unbox emotions and feelings they've spent so long keeping down.

Still, he hadn't expected to hear it from Foggy.

"You're not serious," Ryan said, his eyes narrowing and his voice lowering.

Foggy sighed. "Look, I get that you're all gung-ho about this, and I don't blame you. This is what you do. Hell, you'd probably bleed blue if I cut you. This just isn't my scene, Ryan."

"Your scene?" Ryan asked, his blood already boiling. "This is your sister, Foggy. It's your flesh and blood."

"And she's gone, Ryan!" Foggy shouted, shaking his head. "She's been gone for twenty years. Twenty hard years that I've had to live through. Do you know what her disappearance did to my family, Ryan? Do you have any idea what it put us through? They're my flesh and blood too, you know. They're my family, the people I love. My mother, my father . . . they might not have been murdered, but they died with her."

"All the more reason to look for the person who did this," Ryan said, stunned by the man's hesitancy.

"To what end?" Foggy said, tears welling in his brown eyes, eyes that looked like Haley's. "She's dead and gone. If there's a heaven, I'm sure that's where she went. If not, then what does it matter anyway? The point is, she's at peace now. Why can't we be too?" The breath caught in his throat. "My father is dead. He drank himself into a stupor. My mother, she's as sick as I've ever seen anyone. I don't want her to spend her last days on this earth reliving her worst days. Surely, you can understand that."

Ryan could, but it didn't change anything. "I owe this to her," he answered. "Someone did this to her."

"We don't know that."

"She wouldn't have been there. She wouldn't have been in the marshland of Waverly Plantation on her prom night, Foggy. You know that. If you know who she was going with—"

"I've told you a million times. I don't know. It's terrible that she canceled on you last-minute, but I don't know who she was going with. She didn't say."

"Okay." Ryan took a deep breath. "I'm going to go look around her room, if that's okay?"

"That's why you're here, isn't it?"

Since the moment Haley had vanished, her mother refused to let anyone near her daughter's room, keeping it exactly as it had been the last time she stepped outside. The cold surge of untouched metal ran up his arm as he wrapped his hand around the gold door handle. Taking a deep breath, he opened the door and flipped on the light.

A Red Hot Chili Peppers poster hung on her wall. One he remembered vividly. They'd gone to Charlotte together once just to see the band live in concert. Chaperoned by Ryan's mother, the two spent the entire night dancing and singing along with almost every song before finally managing to sneak away from his mother long enough to steal a few drinks and a quick kiss.

On her dresser was the bright pink glittered telephone she'd convinced her mother to buy, even though she told her it was the most outlandishly ugly thing she'd ever seen. Haley didn't care, though. She knew what she wanted and no one could ever convince her otherwise. They'd spent hours talking to one another after that, though Ryan's own phone was admittedly far less fancy, just something he'd found at the local dollar store. But that didn't matter to him. As long as he could hear Haley's voice on the other end, the young man was happy.

Stepping further into the room and closing the door, he took a seat on her bed, thinking back to the many times he'd sat there before, each time looking into her eyes, each time trying not to stare too long at the curves of her body. But like any red-blooded Southerner, he couldn't help but sneak a peak every now and again, not that Haley seemed to mind, laughing it off each time she caught him looking too long.

He spent the next hour poking through her belongings, each one calling up a different memory, each one peeling back another layer of a time that seemed to have been standing still in that bedroom.

"Well?" Foggy asked as Ryan descended the stairs.

"Nothing."

"Here," Foggy said, handing the detective a small box and a stack of papers. "Maybe you'd like to have these back. I have no use for them."

Holding the unfamiliar papers in his hand and feeling the pain resonate from his friend, Ryan flipped through the pages. "What is this?"

"Your letters." Foggy answered. "My mom found them in Haley's air vent a few weeks after . . . I thought you might like to have them back. The rest is her 'boyfriend box'. Little trinkets you gave her, I guess."

There were a lot of things Ryan wasn't sure about when it came to Haley, but there was one thing he knew for dead-down fact. And that was that he hadn't written these letters. Each one acknowledged feelings of love and desire and each referenced Haley's innocent smile and bright eyes. The words were true, but Ryan Devereux wasn't their author.

"I didn't write these."

"You're the only boy she ever dated for more than a week." Foggy pointed to the letters. "These mention nights out on the beach, riding in cars . . . it had to be you."

"Foggy," the detective answered. "These aren't my letters. I never wrote letters."

Chapter Five

"I just don't know, man," Jackson said. "I don't remember her ever going out with anyone but you. At least not for more than a couple of days. And even then, it was just to piss you off."

"Me neither," Ryan replied.

It had been a few days since he'd been given the letters, and it seemed no matter how many times he read through them, he just couldn't find anything linking an identity. Whoever wrote them, it seemed, was very careful not to leave behind any clues as to who they might be. But to the detective, the whole thing made about as much sense as a cat on a rocking chair.

But what kind of person writes letters and purposefully leaves out such information? Were these letters evidence of premeditation? Had the same person who wrote them ultimately become a killer, or was it just simple coincidence?

"Haley wasn't the kind of girl to keep things quiet," Jackson said. "You remember that time Tanner Knight winked at her? She talked about it for weeks."

Since the two boys were knee-high to a grasshopper, they'd been the best of friends, going through everything the Lowcountry had to offer together. The cold Atlantic waters saw the two boys share many things. It was on the pristine banks of Sullivan's Island where they'd taken their first drink long before it was ever allowed by law. A few years later, the shores of Patriots Point saw Jackson become a man, a few months before his friend and a lifetime before his momma ever approved. Those kinds of things bonded people together, especially in the Deep South where people never stopped knowing their childhood friends.

Jackson Bennett hadn't come from much, living with his momma in a two-room house older and more weathered than some of Charleston County's own oak trees. There'd long been rumors of his momma working the streets down near the docks instead of staying home with her young son. Many nights went by that he'd just end up sleeping over at the Devereux house, staying up all hours of the night with his best friend and talking about big dreams and pretty girls.

Ryan never asked his friend about the rumors, preferring to let sleeping dogs lie, but that hadn't stopped him from wondering where Lydia Bennett was spending her nights. None of that mattered to him, though. They were friends no matter where they came from.

"Why do you think she was dating someone else?" Jackson took another sip of his Jack and Coke.

"Just a theory I'm working on," Ryan answered, keeping the truth of the letters to himself.

Jackson scanned the room. "You here alone?"

"She's not here."

"What? I was just curious." Jackson smiled, scratching his head.

Even though the two men were closer to age forty than age thirty, Jackson Bennett seemed to have maintained his boyish good looks through all those years. With olive skin, deep brown eyes, and a big smile, he'd always been easy on the eyes, but the fact that he'd seemed to stop aging at age twenty-five was something his best friend had always found himself jealous of.

"Yeah, right." Ryan smiled back. "Maybe go shoot up the pharmacy or something. I'm sure she'll find you. Tell you what. I'll give her a call." Ryan pretended to dial his partner.

"No. Ryan, no." Jackson chuckled, trying his best to slap the phone away.

The truth was he needed to get back to work. He was only supposed to stay a few minutes and he'd already been shooting the breeze with his friend for over an hour. Haley's killer was out there somewhere, in all likelihood still walking the streets of Charleston County, and he needed to find them.

He'd managed his guilt, that was true. It took a while, but he'd found a way to keep the weight of the young girl's memory from crushing him under its pressure. Then the thought hit him. What would he say to the person responsible once he'd found them? Would he demand a story, a confession? Would he look for the reason behind their actions and try to understand their truths? Or would he be too angry?

No reason was ever good enough to take someone's life. But how a person could hurt someone so young perplexed him. He'd studied the criminal mind, and he'd gotten to the root of many crimes throughout his career, but senseless cruelty never got any easier to understand.

"All right," Ryan said. "I gotta get back to work."

A few minutes later, the detective was driving toward King Street in the direction of The Savannah Bee Company. It was a small place and a little new to town, but over the last few months, he'd met his partner there almost every day after lunch. There was just something so comforting about the sweet smell of honey wafting through the air. Not to mention the various types of mead they sold, something the detective had managed to grow a liking for after being forced to listen to his partner rattle on about it for so long.

Coming to a small crossroads and taking a look around, Ryan stepped on the accelerator and drove forward. It happened so suddenly he barely even had time to process it. The sound of twisting metal and shattering glass echoed through the silent night. Fragments of his car shot outward onto the side of the road, raining down like rain from an evening thunderstorm.

"Damn!" he said, trying to gather himself.

He felt his car begin to vibrate and shake, and then he saw the lights. Someone, it seemed, decided they were in too big of a rush to pay any attention to the stop sign, deciding instead to crash into the detective's car, and now it seemed like they were trying to leave the scene without saying a word.

"Hey!" he yelled, trying his best to open his jammed door. "Wait!"

It was too late. By the time he'd managed to climb across the seat, they were already headed down highway seventy-eight, melting away into the sweltering southern night. "Shit!" He slammed his hand against the steering wheel.

Ryan stepped out and checked his car for damage. Aside from the door and front fender, it seemed to be in decent shape, though he would have to write a report about this later. Suddenly, a shock of vibration ran through his body and down his leg. Instinctively grabbing for his phone, he pulled it from his pocket and read the screen.

We need to talk.

Chapter Six

"Okay." Ryan sat down. "What did I say?"

This used to be his kitchen, his dinner table, and his wife. But quicker than a flash, he'd lost all three. It wasn't surprising when it happened. In fact, if there was any surprise at all, it was that the marriage had lasted as long as it did.

In the beginning, it was easy. They were in love and still young enough that it seemed like it would be all they needed. But with pressing careers and the stress of daily life and time apart, it became all too clear that the only way either of them would survive this marriage would be to leave it behind.

"Pompous." Jillian answered. "You told our daughter her new father was pompous."

"Referring to him as 'her new father' doesn't make me want to talk about this."

"You know what I mean," she snapped. "My new husband."

"Yes," Ryan replied. "Your new husband. Carly's new stepfather."

"Fine. I'll be more careful with my words. That's good advice for you too, you know."

"I didn't mean anything by it, Jillian. You know that." He sighed. "I don't get that much time with her, you know. She was talking about him. We were laughing and I guess it just slipped out."

"You don't even know Thomas. How can you call him pompous?"

"Cream cheese grits, Jillian," Ryan answered. "The man made cream cheese grits. And besides, who wears a gold bowtie?"

"Keeping tabs on my new husband?"

"More like staying up to date with local news," Ryan clarified. "It just happens to be Thomas who delivers it."

"I want you to stop it. Don't say those things about him. She repeats them and he gets the wrong idea."

Even though they were divorced and she'd moved on and found another man to love, another man to lie by her side as she slept . . . even though she'd found a man to take his place, Ryan Devereux still loved the woman he'd once called his wife. He still found beauty in her smile and kindness in her heart, but they were adults now and that changed things in a way no level of feeling or desire could overcome.

"I spoke to her teacher," Ryan said, looking into her hazel eyes. "She's fighting again."

"I'm working on it. I've spoken to a therapist."

"A therapist?"

"Yes," she said flatly. "I have to do something."

"Have you tried talking to her?"

"Don't give me that," Jillian said, tossing her long dark hair over her right shoulder. "You don't have to deal with her the way I do. Every day, it's something else. Fighting, talking back, stealing—"

"What did she steal?" Ryan asked, surprised by the accusation.

Not that he was an expert by any means, but he'd tried his best to read a few books on how kids handle divorce. He'd even considered therapy once too, just to make dealing with it a little easier. In the end, though, he'd managed to muddle his way through it like any true Lowcountry man—with a few bottles of Jack and some time on the water.

"A cellphone," Jillian answered. "From her teacher's desk drawer."

"She's just lashing out," Ryan said. "She'll be fine. She's a good kid. I don't think she needs therapy."

"She's going," Jillian answered flatly. "I'm her mother."

"What does that mean?"

"It means, I'm her mother."

"This should be *our* decision, Jillian. We should talk this through."

"Doctor Harris comes highly recommended. She's the top family counselor in town."

"I'm sure she's wonderful," Ryan replied. "But this still needs to be something we decide together."

"Why would you object to trying to get our daughter the help she needs?"

"I'm not objecting to helping her. I'm objecting to your making decisions without me," he said, trying his best to hold back the emotions starting to bubble up inside him.

"This would be easier if you'd just get on board." Jillian took a deep breath. "All I'm trying to do is help her. She won't talk to me. She'll barely even look at me. She blames me for what happened."

"She doesn't blame you," Ryan said. "At least, not on purpose. She's a kid. She's confused."

"That's why I'm trying to help her." Jillian placed her hand on his, slowly gliding her finger across his palm.

There'd always been a comfort in her touch. Even now, after the years of history and miles of differences between them, he still couldn't help but almost smile. There'd been a time when he'd have crossed oceans for that woman without even asking why. But times change, and the change affects people in ways they never saw coming.

"When is she supposed to go?" he asked, already feeling a little uneasy with someone poking around in his daughter's head the way therapists do.

"Two weeks."

"I'm taking her out this weekend," Ryan replied after a few silent moments. "I'll talk to her about it then. As long as she's okay with it, I will be too."

"She won't be okay if she thinks you aren't, Ryan. You know that."

"I won't say anything either way. I'll remain neutral. I promise you."

Co-parenting a child was no easy task, especially while having to navigate the minefield of divorce along with it. But for all their mistakes, missteps, and misunderstandings, the two seemed to be doing okay.

"Stay," she said, seeing Ryan begin to rise from his chair. "Just for a few minutes. I'll pour some wine."

He gave a wicked smile. "What about Thomas?"

"He's not going to be home for a little while. Besides, I doubt he'd have much to say. We're parenting."

The two exes spent the next forty-five minutes just shooting the breeze. They covered everything from Ida Randolph's alleged involvement with her sister's husband to Mike Smith and his penchant for stepping out on his new wife, all the while not talking about much of anything. But that just seemed to be the way of conversation in the Old South. Give people just a little bit of gossip and a warm summer breeze and they were just as happy as two pigs in the mud.

But like all easy conversation, it finally reached a sudden and abrupt end when Detective Devereux answered a phone call from an old friend, one that would send him back to Haley King's house for the second time in as many days.

"What's the matter?" Jillian asked, sitting upright in her chair.

"It's the King house, out on Johns Island," he answered. "It's been broken into."

"All right," she said as he stood and headed for the door. "Be safe. And don't forget, you've got dessert this Sunday."

Chapter Seven

"About time," Kit said as her partner stepped out of his car. "What happened? You hit a gator?"

"I was headed to meet Jillian. Hit and run."

"You know who?" She raised an eyebrow.

"No. They were long gone by the time my car started. I got no plates, nothing. I think it was a silver or white SUV."

"That's some damn good police work right there."

"Doesn't matter," he replied. "Just a few dents and a busted headlight. I'll get it fixed."

"You sure you're ready to be back?"

"I'm fine," he snapped. "I put out an APB on any light-colored SUV with front-end damage. We'll find them."

That was true. Ryan Devereux was a fine detective, and if anyone could find someone with so little to go on, it was him. There were a million different kinds of criminals hiding in Charleston County's thick marshlands, but they all knew one simple truth. They all made mistakes sooner or later, and all Ryan needed to do was be there when they did.

"I'm sure of it," Kit answered. "The owner tells me you were here yesterday?"

"Yes," he replied. "The body in the marsh was his sister."

"Right," she said. "King. Were you able to get anything?"

"Nothing," He replied, feeling a drop of sweat roll down his forehead.

It happened the same way every year. Winter gave way to spring, then spring hung around for a little while, sending thunderstorms rolling down South Carolina's splendid countryside. But then, almost instantly and with no more notice than a mosquito, summer came biting at you like an angry gator. Damp, hot humidity licked the detective's skin, trapping hot air under his cotton shirt with every step. Even though he'd spent his life in this heat, there was still something difficult about those first few summer days.

"Okay," Ryan said, sitting down across from Foggy. "Start at the beginning." His hair was a little messier than usual and there was a wide gash near his right temple, which he held a wet washcloth over. Aside from that, he seemed pretty unaffected by the situation.

"I'd just gotten home from the bar." He brought a glass of Jack Daniels to his lips. "When I put my key in the door I realized it was unlocked. I made my way from room to room looking for anything out of the ordinary."

"Does anyone else have a key to this house?" Kit asked. "Maybe a girlfriend, a family member?"

"No," Foggy answered, the wet cloth reddening with traces of blood. "I have the only key. I was heading into the kitchen when I heard something upstairs. I went to her room. At first, I didn't see anything, but then someone popped out from behind the door and clocked me in the head. I fell. By the time I got downstairs, they'd already made it outside."

"Was anything taken?"

"No." He sighed. "Not that I can see."

"Did you hear any vehicles or see which way they went?" Kit asked.

"No, but . . ."

Ryan leaned in. "But what?"

"When I passed the Angel Oak, there was an SUV there. Then later, after I drove around looking for the guy, it was gone."

"The Angel Oak is one of the most popular tourist sites in South Carolina," Kit replied. "There are always people visiting."

"Yes," Foggy responded. "But I've seen this car before. Plus, it had South Carolina plates. Locals don't visit the tree this time of year, only tourists. You know that."

"That's not much to go on," Kit said.

"I'll make a note of it," Ryan interjected. "You said they were in Haley's room, right?"

"This is your fault!" Foggy turned to Ryan. "Someone was in her room because you couldn't keep your mouth shut. You couldn't let the dead rest in peace. My sister has been gone for twenty years and now you're bringing her back up. Do you have any idea what that's like?"

"I know you don't want us here, but we need to see the room," Ryan replied.

"You know the way." Foggy waved his hand, then dabbed his wound again. "Be quick!"

Ryan and Kit headed up the spiral staircase and onto the small second-floor landing as Foggy waited downstairs. Perhaps it was the fact that he'd gotten used to living on a boat, but the house itself seemed much too big to be lived in by just one person, even if that person was as large as Foggy King. Big vacant spaces just seemed to have a way of making people seem lonely, or at least that had always been Ryan Devereux's experience.

"It looks untouched," Kit said, looking around Haley's bedroom. "Like it's frozen in time."

"It is untouched," Ryan answered. "They left it this way after she . . ."

"Right."

"I was in here just yesterday. It looks exactly the same now as it did then."

"Maybe they were just looking to score some cash or something."

"But nothing was taken," the detective replied. "This was something else. I can feel it."

"All right," she said. The tone in her voice was no surprise. Kit Walker preferred facts over feelings any day of the week, and she'd be the first to tell you. "What do you think it was, if not a robbery?"

"I don't know," Ryan answered. "But this is a nice house on Johns Island. Not a lot of break-ins around here. This has something to do with Haley. I know it."

"The rest of the house is untouched. That does back up your theory, but this is a cold case from twenty years ago." Kit opened a small jewelry box, then placed it back on the dresser. "Tell me about it."

"What?" Ryan wrinkled his forehead.

"Tell me about prom night." Kit folded her arms across her chest. "I just know you two had a date and then she canceled at the last minute."

"That's really all there is."

"That's never all there is. You know that. I bet you haven't talked the night out in quite some time. It might help."

She was right about that part. Ryan Devereux wasn't really a 'spill your guts' kind of man. He'd never been the type of guy to lay his head in someone else's lap and cry over failed relationships or stressful situations. To him, it was more important to keep himself together and actually do something about it.

"She canceled on me about three hours before the prom." Ryan cleared his throat. "I had no idea why. She wouldn't say. She was upset, though, so I assumed she was staying home. We fought about it but she got mad and hung up the phone. That's all."

"If she wasn't going, then why was she wearing that dress when we found her?"

"Later that night, her parents came to my house. They were looking for her. They said she'd left the house and headed to the school. They had no idea she'd canceled on me." Ryan pulled back the purple lace curtains, not sure what he was looking for.

"So, she did go to the prom?"

"No. I mean . . . I don't know." He looked back at his partner. Talking about it was actually a little harder than he'd imagined it would be. Not that as a Carolina boy, he wasn't used to talking, but there was still pain there, pain he got from feeling like he hadn't done enough to save her. "No one at the prom saw her. No one except for Shirley Baker."

"Let's speak with her."

"We can't." He cleared his dry throat. "She was the assistant principal. She passed away about three years ago. But I've spoken with her a few times before. She said she saw Haley in the hallway just as the dance was about to begin, but no one could ever back that up."

Chapter Eight

"I reckon you're pretty torn up about all of this, boy," Ryan's uncle said, tossing him a cold Corona.

Pauley Wells would be spending the next week living aboard *Second Wind*, sleeping in the back room of his nephew's houseboat while the bar he both owned and lived above was fumigated for an especially invasive and tough set of beetles. Something not all too out of the ordinary in the Lowcountry.

It didn't bother the detective too much, though. He was happy for the company, and Lord knows, his Uncle Pauley knew how to carry on a conversation as well as anyone in South Carolina. He'd always been close to the man, especially given the fact that his own dad was always stationed so far away.

But like most every family in the South, his momma made sure he still had someone in his life to teach him how to hunt and fish and just be a man. It was his uncle, with his booming voice and love of the water, who'd first taught the young boy how to sail. But more than that, he taught him to love and respect the place he'd come from and the history that created it.

Being a man in the South is a special thing, especially when you turn out to be a good one. Kind and strong, tough and loving, a true Southern gentleman was something you could search the world over and still not find its equal. At least, that's what his momma always told him.

"I'm okay," Ryan replied. "It's been twenty years. I've had my chance to process it, to deal with my emotions and put them where they belong."

"Deal with your emotions. Put them where they belong." Pauley's head snapped back. "Boy, I think you've been watching too much television."

"What?"

"What kind of crap is that?" he snapped. "I remember the way you talked about that girl, the way you spoke about marrying her one day and living beside the water. Don't you remember?"

"Yes," Ryan answered. "I remember, but that was a long time ago."

"Don't make no difference," Pauley said. "Why, whenever that girl disappeared, you were fit to be tied."

"I was upset, yes. But I handled it the best way I could."

"You did a fine job handling it." His uncle threw back a long sip of his beer.

"Then what is this?"

"This is me asking if you're okay." He set the bottle on the floor next to him.

"I'm fine."

Warm Atlantic air blew in from the south, bringing with it fresh new hope for the next day, in addition to bringing a bit of much-needed fresh air into Ryan's boat. The summer sun is an especially hot thing in its own regard, but couple that with one hundred percent humidity and the air felt almost too thick to breathe at times.

Ryan had purchased his Bravada houseboat from a police auction down in Jacksonville a few weeks after he and Jillian decided to call it quits. In truth, it was a little newer, a little nicer, and a little flashier than he'd normally go for. But he'd managed to get it for next to nothing after being confiscated from some cybersecurity tycoon with a penchant for money laundering.

It was easy, quick, and new enough to basically be problem-free. It just lacked a bit of character, that's all. But with twin seventy-five-horsepower engines, a mostly fiberglass exterior, and a pretty low operating cost, the deal was just too good to pass up. Besides, he was pretty sure he'd be able to add a bit of character once he'd taken her out a few times.

For the most part, he was right. She sailed like a dream, with an easiness that reminded him of the way his momma's big Cadillac would glide across those old South Carolina roadways. Watching the bright sun melt into the ocean as it stretched out into infinity right in front of him was a feeling that never seemed to get old and never seemed to repeat. Each night brought a new color to the sky, each wave a new song as it crashed against the shore. With the water at his front and the Lowcountry at his back, Ryan Devereux was content in a way some people could only dream of.

"What are you thinking about, Sonny?" Pauley asked. "You've been staring out the window for half an hour now."

Ryan looked at the man he'd known all his life, seeing the weathered wrinkles on his face that came from a lifetime on the water. He listened to the raspy broken sound of his voice, the one that came from breathing in that thick Carolina air, and he began to wonder, was this his future?

"Do you think much about her?" Ryan asked. "Aunt Rose, I mean. Do you ever wonder what it would be like if she were still here?"

It was rare the two ever talked about the woman. Ryan wasn't even sure why he was doing it now. There was just something about the sound of the ocean and the warm mist on his face that seemed to drop his inhibitions just enough to broach the kinds of subjects he usually distanced himself from.

"I think about her when I head into town," Pauley said, his deep, broken voice drifting away, getting lost somewhere over the ocean. "I think about her when it's hot and when it rains. I think about her when I get my medicine filled and when I wake up with no one next to me. But no, I don't wonder what it would like it she were around. That wouldn't be fair to her memory. She fought long and hard, and I won't take that away from her. She can finally rest now."

Rose Wells had been a strong woman all her life, planting crops, digging fields, and raising her babies, all while making time for her family and for the Lord. Ryan remembered his mother saying she was stronger than a mule and twice as easy to talk to. But like so many other good people, she'd been struck by a disease that ate her away from the inside out. The once strong woman just seemed to suddenly fade away until finally breathing her last breath just as the Christmas lights came down and a fresh new calendar appeared on the wall.

"I wasn't trying to upset you," Ryan said. "I was just thinking maybe you were lonely or something. Like maybe you'd like to try and meet someone."

"Listen, boy." Pauley focused his eyes on the edge of the dock. "That woman did right by me, and for whatever time I have left in this world, I'm sure as cotton gonna do right by her."

"Okay."

He'd heard that tone before, the one that let him know his uncle simply wasn't interested in whatever nonsense the boy was spouting. And just like every other time, he backed off, letting the conversation fall by the wayside.

"I need to shower," Ryan said, trying to break the conversation. "Tomorrow is Saturday. I've got dinner with Mr. Abernathy."

"I'll never understand why you still have dinner with your old chemistry teacher."

"He always took an interest in me. He always took time to help me through classes."

"It's just a little strange, that's all. Not something you see every day."

"Strange?" Ryan chuckled. "Well now, if that ain't the pot calling the kettle black."

"What about that niece of mine?" Pauley asked as Ryan began to stand. "Heard from her lately?"

"Not in a few weeks," Ryan replied. "Last we spoke, she was supposed to be heading back home after the summer. Apparently, that new husband she's got doesn't take too well to the southern humidity."

"Psh," Pauley scoffed. "Well, I guess she's old enough that her wants won't hurt her."

"I guess so."

Chapter Nine

Opened in 1987, Hyman's Seafood had been a beloved Charleston institution for much of Ryan's life. Honestly, though, over the last few years, it had seemed to garner the reputation of a tourist trap more than a local hangout. That didn't mean the piping-hot hushpuppies or flaky fried shrimp were any less delicious. It just meant Ryan and his former professor would have to wait in line a little longer to get them.

Finally sitting down at his table, he noticed a little plaque in front of the neighboring table which read, *Sarah Jessica Parker ate at this table.* Such plaques were scattered across the restaurant, dropping names like Bill Clinton and The Beach Boys. It was a nice enough touch of character, though the detective couldn't imagine anyone truly cared about such things.

Across from him sat his former teacher, Rufus Abernathy, the man who'd at once inspired him and challenged him. It was Mr. Abernathy who'd first suggested law enforcement to the young student after noticing his penchant for finding the truth in people's words. It wasn't only Ryan whom the man helped, however. Rufus was just one of those teachers everyone loved.

"What looks good?" Rufus asked through a neatly-trimmed silver goatee.

"I'm gonna go basic," Ryan said, closing his menu. "Lowcountry boil. What about you?"

"Fried shrimp. You can't go wrong with a classic."

With its weathered brick exterior, dark wooden floors, and big picture windows, the restaurant created a wonderful atmosphere for shooting the breeze with an old friend. The loud clangs of forks and knives scraping across plates filled the room, trying their best to drown out the echoes of conversation flowing through the upstairs dining area.

"So . . ." the professor said, looking up through his thick glasses, his bushy dark eyebrows almost touching the rims. "How are things going with your work? Now that you're back."

"Well enough," Ryan answered. "The last few days have been hard, though." The detective paused, taking a deep breath. "Haley Kings's body was discovered."

Mr. Abernathy's eyes widened. "Haley King. I haven't watched the news in a few days. I haven't heard that name in quite some time. I wasn't aware the case was still active."

"It wasn't," Ryan replied. "Until we found her body, that is. Now it's been sent to cold case—to me."

"How stressful that must be for you." Rufus pulled a lemon from his glass, squeezing it into his sweet tea. "I know the two of you were an item."

"It hasn't been the best."

"Are there any leads in what may have happened to her?"

"We're working a few different angles," Ryan replied. "But . . . let's not talk about that right now."

"Sure." Rufus took a long sip of his iced tea. "I was just checking to make sure you were alright."

"I'm okay."

Conversation began to flow between the two men like the waters of the Ashley River. Much like every time they ate together, the men shared stories and memories, oftentimes small and insignificant, other times a little deeper than it seemed either of them had set out for. Tonight, however, it seemed no matter where the conversation began, it always led back to the same place.

"Have you spoken to her brother?" Rufus asked.

"Yes." Ryan shuffled uncomfortably in his wooden chair. "A couple of different times, actually. He's less than thrilled with the idea of us reopening the investigation. He gave me a box of things though. Just random trinkets from her childhood. I don't recognize half of them. He didn't say much about it. Like I said, he's not happy with me."

"I can't say I blame him," the professor answered. "I remember hearing the way the murder tore that family apart. I doubt they need to go through it again. Besides, I'm sure the guilty party has had time to repent."

"Time to repent?" Ryan's forehead wrinkled. "To hell with them. Who cares? Someone killed a girl. They took her life with their own hands and they should be held accountable. Why can't I get anyone to see that?"

"Whoa." Rufus held out a hand. "I didn't mean to upset you, Ryan. I was only trying to point out that it's been a very long time since Haley went missing. Digging around now can only upset an already fragile situation."

"You're the one who told me to find the truth in everything. It was you who inspired me to become a detective. How can you look me in the face and tell me not to do everything I can to bring her killer to justice?"

"I'm sorry." Rufus sat up a little straighter in his chair. "This is a tough situation for everyone. I can't imagine how you must be feeling."

"I was curious about one thing—"

"Would you excuse me?" Rufus said as his phone began to ring. "I'll be right back."

As the night began to melt away and the dinner crowd began to lessen, Detective Devereux looked out the large picture window next to his table and watched the cars below him pass by. Downtown Charleston was always crowded on the weekend, especially in the summer. Tonight was no exception. Tourists young and old walked the picturesque streets, sipping drinks, laughing, and carrying on, living the kind of life most locals took for granted.

"Erma Bombeck ate at this table," he muttered to himself, reading the plaque in front of his professor's empty seat. *"Who's Erma Bombeck?"*

"An author," Rufus said, coming in from around the corner. "She wrote a few bestsellers after becoming known from a newspaper column, I think." He removed his wallet from his back pocket. "I'm sorry, Ryan. I need to go."

"Oh. No," Ryan said, holding his hand out. "I'll take care of this."

"No. You got the last one. It's my turn."

Stepping out onto the red brick sidewalk of Meeting Street, Ryan took a breath, letting the thick, hot air of his hometown fill his lungs. To the tourists passing by, glistening with sweat and fanning themselves with paper, it must have seemed like one of the hottest nights they'd ever felt. But to the native South Carolinian, it was the beginning of summer, and with the storms brewing in the Atlantic and the humidity on the rise, he knew it would only get hotter.

With its own culture, geography, architecture, economy, and even cuisine, a night in Lowcountry was like a night nowhere else. People came from across the world to experience it firsthand. With shrimp boats, palmetto trees, and big front porches with rocking chairs and pitchers of sweet tea around every corner, what's not to love about Lowcountry? Lots of places are famous for things, but to Ryan Devereux, nowhere deserved that fame more than the sub-tropical land he called home.

"You have yourself a good night, now. You hear?" A middle-aged woman said, closing the door behind him.

"Yes, ma'am," he replied, heading for his car. Until that moment, Ryan had managed to have a pretty nice evening, but turning the corner away from Meeting Street, what he saw next made him madder than a wet hen.

"What the . . ." he muttered, seeing the damage done to his car.

Shattered glass lay on the ground in every direction caused by busted windows, tail lights, and side mirrors. Large dents littered the hood and side doors. The damn thing looked as though it had been attacked by some sort of angry buffalo or something. But most alarming of all was the bright yellow piece of paper taped to the rear driver's-side window, the only one left untouched.

The note was a threat of sorts, telling the detective to drop his investigation or be met with an even worse fate than the girl he was investigating. The handwriting was a mess, slanting in every direction with ink drips along the bottom of the paper. It looked to the seasoned investigator as though whoever wrote it was in one hell of a hurry.

"Charleston County Police Department," the voice on the line said.

"This is Detective Devereux," Ryan said into his phone. "I've got an issue."

Chapter Ten

"Maybe you should just let it go," Jillian said, plopping a bowl of mashed potatoes down on the table with just a little too much force.

Sunday dinner was something Ryan Devereux still ate with his daughter, ex-wife, and her new fiancé. During the divorce, it sounded like a good idea, and it usually turned out okay. But other times, like this one, he wished he'd have just skipped the meal altogether.

"I can't just let it go," Ryan answered. "And Lord knows, I wish people would stop suggesting it. This is my job."

"It's dangerous, Ryan," Jillian answered. "There are two schools of thought in this town. Either Foggy killed her, or someone else did, someone no one knows about. Either way, that killer is still walking these streets. And if they're threatening you, maybe hold up. The case is twenty years old."

Having been to church earlier that morning, Jillian was decked out in her Sunday best. A long-on-one-side white dress with large purple orchids climbing upward hung almost to the floor as she stood next to her ex-husband, placing a bowl of green beans down beside him. Rising above the smell of fresh fried chicken and baking bread was the scent of her perfume.

Peony, magnolia, and lotus flower topped off with just a hint of amber . . . it was always the same scent. Jillian was a creature of habit first and foremost. Once she found something she liked, she usually stuck with it. Unless, of course, that thing was Ryan Devereux, though to be fair, she did insist that he join them every Sunday after mass.

"Danger is the job," he answered. "It's all dangerous. It always has been. This isn't anything new. Twenty years isn't so long in cold-case anyway."

"That's right," Thomas chimed in. "You can't let that stop you from doing your job. I mean . . . just take a look at soldiers. They risk their lives. Even reporters go into dangerous situations when chasing stories. But you just have to keep the course sometimes."

Well, now, if that ain't something . . . Ryan thought to himself. *Is this asshole actually comparing himself to a soldier?*

Thomas Kent was one of the most infuriatingly self-absorbed people south of the Mason-Dixon line. With his bleach-white smile, perfectly coiffed hair, and a laugh fake enough that you could probably buy it at the store, Ryan could barely stand to be in the same room with the man, let alone share a meal. But for the sake of his daughter, he managed to swallow his pride every weekend and spend a few hours listening to him blow wind in his own sails.

"Yes . . . something like that."

"I'm just saying," Jillian said, finally taking a seat at the table. "Why not give the case to another officer? Why not someone who doesn't have as strong a connection as you? You were in love with the girl, for God's sake. It makes me nervous."

"Nervous?" he asked. "Why on earth would that make you nervous?"

"You don't get it, do you?" she said, slowly placing her fork back on the table. "What it's like to worry about someone not coming home that night. Worrying about . . . I thought when they moved you to cold case, you'd be sitting behind a desk. That you'd be . . ."

"Be what?" Ryan asked. "Irrelevant?" He didn't say it, but that was also how he felt most of the time sitting around this very table. Irrelevant.

"Safe," she said. "I mean, is cold case even what you want?"

"What?" he asked. "I . . . cold case is good, I guess."

"You guess?" she snapped. "You always said the only thing you wanted to do was be a detective. You always said you didn't want to sit behind a desk. That you weren't cut out for it. You said you were going to leave the force and start your own private investigation firm."

"I'm not behind a desk," Ryan answered.

"But you should be!" she snapped.

"Why are you doing this?" He leaned in, his face hovering above the steaming hot fried chicken.

"Doing what?"

"This!" he said. "Trying to start a fight. Trying to make me feel like I've made the wrong choice . . . again."

Jillian took a deep breath and then something changed behind her eyes. The storm that had been brewing in those bright blue orbs settled into something dark, something almost mournful.

"Was it a choice?" she asked. "Or did you give up?"

"Give up on what?" he asked, though he already knew the answer.

"On me!" Her eyes welled with tears. "On us! You were supposed to start the business. You would have been home at five, and we would have had dinner. We would have been a family, and everything would have been fine. You weren't supposed to be on the street."

Ryan's eyes flickered over to Thomas, though there was little he could read on the stoic reporter's face.

"I was helping people who needed me. I still am." Frustration rose in Ryan's voice.

"I needed you . . ." Her voice trailed off. "Your daughter needed you."

Her words cut deeper than any knife ever could. Ryan may have been a lot of things, but a bad father wasn't one of them. He'd cherished that little girl since the first moment he held her, since the first time her saw her little eyes open and look up at him with that sense of wonder only a new baby can deliver.

"How could you say that to me?" he asked, sitting back in his chair. "How could you say that in front of her? We were young. Sacrifices had to be made."

"Your child is not a sacrifice!" she screamed.

"Don't you dare paint me as that person, Jilly," he said.

"Don't call me that," she answered, her wide eyes filling with tears. "You don't get to call me that ever again."

"And you don't get to rewrite history. Things weren't as black and white as you're making them out to be. You were home raising a baby and I was doing the only thing I knew how to do. I put food on our table and clothes on our backs." Ryan felt his throat begin to swell. "Maybe I didn't make it home in time for dinner, but I was only doing what I thought I was supposed to. For you, for our daughter. There's no wrong in that, Jillian."

"This was never about food on the table or clothes on our backs," Jillian spat. "You could have worked with my father. He begged you to take over the company. This is about your caring more about some face on a milk carton than the woman you swore to love, than the daughter you brought into the world. It's about the fact that you're addicted to this chase, to the danger."

"You used to say that's what you loved about me," he answered.

"Yeah," she muttered. "Well, it used to be true. Now it's just sad."

As an uncomfortable silence fell over the dinner table, Ryan excused himself and headed to the restroom. He needed to get away, to breathe, even if only for a moment. Maybe there would be Advil in the bathroom, perhaps even a shot of whiskey somewhere along the way. Anything to take the edge off.

Closing the door behind him and looking at his slightly weathered reflection, he wondered for a moment if she was right. Had he really been so absent, so preoccupied with work that he'd missed all the signs? Raising a baby alone was hard work, he was sure of it. But in the South, men worked and women stayed home. At least, that's what he'd been told before he knew differently.

But did that mean the blame all lay with him? Couldn't she have explained this to him sooner, before everything went to hell? Or had she tried? Maybe he was too caught up in the idea of what a family was supposed to be to see what it actually was. At this point, he wasn't sure. The only thing he knew was that his head was pounding and he wanted this dinner to be over.

Kneeling down, he opened the cabinet under the sink, remembering he'd once found the ibuprofen there. Then, just when he thought his head couldn't get any more crowded, he saw something that truly threw him for a loop. There, folded under the sink, was a love letter. Alone, that might have not been such an odd thing. What was odd, though, was the use of a nickname he'd seen only a few days before on a very similar letter.

I love you, Pookiepie.

Chapter Eleven

If Ryan had to use only one word to describe the city he called home, it would be beloved. That's why even the thought that someone who was dangerous enough to murder a young girl and make threats against him might be sleeping down the hall from his daughter made his stomach turn. This was Lowcountry. These types of people weren't supposed to be in his life. They were supposed to be behind bars.

Slowly driving through the meandering backroads of South Carolina, you met good people, the kind of people who took time out of their day to stop and speak with you. Folks in Lowcountry are engaging, kind, and generally curious about other folks, asking where you're going and what you're up to. It seemed now, though, that he'd have to ask Thomas Kent those same questions, but for a much different reason than friendly curiosity.

"All right." Kit Walker plopped herself down at the bar. "Tell me what's going on."

It wasn't often that Ryan Devereux found himself unnerved by things, but seeing that note in the bathroom certainly threw him for a loop. Someone obviously didn't like the idea of the detective reopening this cold case to the point that they were willing to threaten him. If that person turned out to be his daughter's new stepfather, well . . . that dog just wasn't going to hunt.

"I found this note." He handed it to her in a sealed plastic bag as the soft echo of his daughter's laughter came barreling in from the shore while she splashed near the water's edge.

Keeping plastic gloves and a few small bags in his pocket was something the detective had been doing since his early days on the force. Evidence seemed to always turn up in the oddest of places, usually when you were least expecting it, and this time was no different. What began as a simple Sunday dinner had quickly morphed into what may very well be an investigation into a murderer.

"Pookiepie . . ." Kit bit the side of her lip, catching the similarity immediately. "It's the same nickname."

"Yes," Ryan answered. "Only this one is written to my wife, and it's signed by Thomas Kent."

"Have you checked the handwriting?" she asked, tracing her eyes around each letter.

"I looked. There are similarities. But the Haley King notes were written twenty years ago. This sounds recent. Handwriting changes over time."

"I know that," she answered, looking up at her partner. "Let forensics take a look. If it's there, they'll find it."

"I will, but it will take them days, maybe weeks. If my daughter is living in the house with a murderer, I need to know. Especially one that's been put on edge."

"What are you getting at?" she asked.

"You," he answered. "They've only met you a couple of times. And Lord knows, Thomas is so self-involved I doubt he'd even remember you."

"You want me to tail your ex-wife's new husband?" she asked.

"No," he replied. "I know I can't ask you to do that. It would be unprofessional. But if I just so happen to mention where the sonofabitch was going to be tomorrow and you happened to find yourself there coincidentally . . ."

"Coincidentally?" Kit asked, a sly smile spreading across her face.

"That's what I said," Ryan answered.

"Let me ask you something," she said, looking across the small outdoor bar and into the endless blue Atlantic. "Do you think he killed Haley?"

"I don't know. I've spent the last little while thinking about that. I don't ever remember her mentioning his name or anything. But someone killed her, and at the moment, this note is the best link we have. Besides, even if the chance is small, it's still my daughter in that house with him."

The thick summer heat caused the once-stiff collar of his shirt to wilt and fall forward. Sweat pooled on his forehead, rolling down his face in heavy tracks. A cool wind blew in from the ocean, sending a chill across his body as it landed on his moisture-covered skin. It was only in the Deep South that a man could at once sweat like a sinner in church while shivering like a fish in the stream.

"I'll do a little digging," Kit said, "to see if I can find a connection. But you need to stay away from this. Away from Thomas Kent. Let me do the heavy lifting. You know, hypothetically."

"Hypothetically?" he asked.

"That's what I said," she answered, smiling again.

"I will," he said, not completely sure he believed his own words.

Kit Walker finished off the last of her Corona and headed back toward the parking lot. Ryan turned his stool outward, watching his daughter and her friend enjoy themselves. He couldn't help but feel something rise within him as he watched her, a visceral mix of anger and fear at the chance that someone would threaten her.

It was her birth that had changed his life so much. It was hearing her cry and watching her grow that forced him to become a man even before he was ready. He loved her in the truest of senses. Carly Devereux meant the world to her father, and in his eyes, she was the most beautiful, kind, and sweet child to ever grace those southern shores.

"Dad." Carly tapped his arm. "Someone told me to give you this." She smiled, handing him a letter.

Ryan's eyes grew wide as he looked down to see what amounted to a threat on his life written across the paper. The note warned him against continuing the investigation and the dangers it would bring to both him and his family.

"Who gave you this?" He leapt from his stool, scanning the shoreline.

"A man," Carly replied. "He said he was your friend and that it was important."

"Did he touch you? Did he threaten you?"

"Dad . . ." the young girl said. "What are you talking about?"

"Who gave you the letter, Carly?"

"I told you, I don't know! What's wrong?" she said, her bottom lip beginning to shake. "Who was he? What does the letter say?"

"Come on," Ryan said, grabbing the two girls' arms. "We're going home."

For as inviting, peaceful, and friendly as he'd seen the Carolina backroads his whole life, Ryan Devereux now felt betrayed by the miles of marsh and swampland stretching out around him. It was as though the night and the people it camouflaged in its darkness were now a danger to the life of someone he held dear.

The tires of his car screamed as he turned down the small, winding driveway to his wife's house. He just needed his daughter home and safe in her bed so that he could figure out what in hell's half-acre was going on and who'd gotten too close to his daughter.

"What's the matter?" Jillian asked, stepping out and seeing the look on his face.

"Nothing," he answered. "I just have a few things to do. Can you please make sure she stays inside?"

"Why?" Jillian asked. "Ryan, tell me what's going on."

"I'll explain later," he said. "I need to bring something to the station. Just keep an eye on Carly." He kissed his daughter's forehead. "See you later, baby."

Chapter Twelve

As the morning sun streaked across his houseboat, Ryan woke from an unsettling dream. Haley King called out to him in the night, her words drowned out by the water in her lungs as she sank deeper and deeper into the thick, hot marshland. She begged him to find her true killer, to bring justice to her memory and take whoever was responsible for this tragedy off the street before they came after him.

Ryan woke to the feeling of strangling as the sensation of water invading his lungs swept over him like a hot Lowcountry breeze. It was his official job to solve crime, but it was his God-given duty to protect the lives of his family. Either way, whoever was responsible for this crime, whoever was threatening him, they would soon come face to face with not only a detective but a father too.

"There we go . . ." he muttered to himself, watching as Thomas Kent left his driveway and headed toward downtown Charleston.

There was just something about the man he didn't trust, about the way he spoke and carried himself. After all, anyone that self-obsessed likely wouldn't have to think twice about hurting a young girl. Especially if he'd done it before.

Ryan followed him down Charleston's bustling Queen Street toward the local news station where he worked. He parked across the street and watched him enter. Not taking the chance on going into the building, he decided to park across the street and wait a little while. It was almost time for the morning news, Thomas's favorite part of the day, or so Ryan had been told.

Unlocking his phone, he tuned into the local television app, the one Thomas insisted he download in order to see his broadcasts. The thing had been on his phone for over a year and he'd only ever used it once, preferring not to watch Thomas bask in the glory of himself at eight o'clock in the morning. This time, though, Ryan was actually interested in what he had to say.

He spoke of everything from the storm slowly making its way up the coast to some outlandish comment he'd heard the president make a few days before. He covered basically everything that had gone on in their little southern belle of a town, with one glaring exception—Haley King.

The girl's name never left his lips, not once. You'd think a case as famous as hers would have made the cut, at least around here. But no. He just kept prattling on about everything else, all the while smiling into the camera like he'd just bought it dinner.

A half hour later, the program reached its end, an event which hadn't come a second too soon for Ryan. Even on the off-chance he wasn't responsible for everything that was going on, the detective still hated watching him. It wasn't jealousy, though. Not at all. Truth be told, Ryan was happy his wife had decided to move on. Not only did that make it okay for him to do so as well, but it also meant that maybe she'd finally found what she'd been looking for.

"Hey," the detective whispered to himself. "Where are you going?"

Looking out his side window, he watched as Thomas Kent exited the news station and headed down a small alley. Maybe it was just dumb luck, or maybe it was the grace of God, but from his particular location, Ryan didn't need to move his car or even step outside to get a clean view of where Thomas was headed.

"Who the hell is that?" he muttered again, watching Thomas meet with a man he didn't recognize. They spoke for a few minutes, then Thomas handed him what looked like a small stack of cash.

Was it a drug deal? Had he just witnessed a crime taking place? Or was it something else entirely? Perhaps this was the man who'd defaced the detective's car, or perhaps Mr. Kent had paid him to shatter the glass and ruin the hood. He wasn't sure. Instinct told him to intervene, to march up to them and make himself known. If whatever was happening was illegal, they'd have nowhere to go, nowhere to hide. But like he'd done so many times before, the detective ignored his instincts, instead choosing to stay back and see where the road led.

"Ryan!" A voice yelled out as his driver's side door opened.

"Jillian. What are you doing here?"

"Carly left her phone in here. I tracked—" She stopped, looking down the alley and seeing her fiancé. "What are you doing?"

"I was—"

"You're watching Thomas, aren't you?" she snapped, her voice deepening a little. "Why?"

"I'm just doing a little investigating," he answered.

"Investigating my fiancé?" she asked. "You have no right!"

"Yes," he answered. "I do. I have the right as an officer and I have the right as a father."

"A father?" Jillian's eyes widened. "What does Carly have to do with anything?"

"This man lives in the house with my daughter, Jillian," Ryan answered, growing a little tired of her accusatory tone. "Do you really think I won't try to protect her?"

"Protect her from what, Ryan?" she asked, stepping onto the pavement. "This is about my moving on, isn't it? This is about my getting married again. You're jealous."

"No!" Ryan replied. "That has nothing to do with this. I'm happy for you."

"Like hell you are," she said. "Don't you think I see the way you look at Thomas, the way you roll your eyes and purse your lips when you speak to him?"

"I didn't say I was in love with the guy, Jillian," Ryan responded. "I just said I wasn't jealous of him. Which, believe me, I'm not!"

"Then what?" She threw her arms up. "What is it?"

"I told you," Ryan answered. "I'm working."

The two once-lovers had been through this song and dance a million times over, each one trying to prove out a point and one of them usually not being completely forthcoming with information. It was simply old-hat. That is, until what happened next.

"Ryan!" His ex-wife said, marching around the front of the car. "Tell me what's going on right now!"

"I'm not going to do that," he said, slowing his words. "I won't let you involve yourself in an open investigation."

"Tell me why you're spying on Thomas!" She threw a slap his way.

"Jillian. I've told—" His words were cut short as he grabbed her arm and held it in place.

Physical altercations were never the detective's favorite thing, and for the most part, he managed to steer clear of them. At least until his ex-wife's new fiancé lost control and punched him in the nose while a crowd of onlookers stood only a few feet away.

"Hey, man!" Thomas said. "Take your hands off her!"

The metallic taste of blood crept into his mouth, dripping from his nose and down his shirt. In the nineteen years they'd known one another, the two had argued many times, but never had they come close to getting physical. But as pain pulsated through his face, Ryan could only think maybe it's true what they say. Maybe time really does change everything.

"You punched me," he said, hearing the sound of sirens in the distance.

Chapter Thirteen

Chief Evans walked into the interrogation room with all the patience and grace of a hungry bulldog bouncing around a cage. Ryan's superior officer, Evans was a large man with dark skin, a mustache, and a balding head that gleamed against the fluorescent light filling the room. He huffed at Ryan, barely looking at him as he sat across the table.

This was a strange turn of events for the detective. Usually, he could be found on the other side of this table, asking questions and digging for information from the lowest-caliber people the Carolina Lowcountry had to offer. It was different today, though, and the look of intense fury on Chief Evans's face said that the older man was relishing this moment.

To say that Evans had never been a fan of Ryan was like saying the South never got over losing the Civil War. It went unspoken. Ryan had been something of a troublemaker in his younger years, sowing his wild oats and all of that. His first interaction with Evans was way back when the man was known as *Officer* Evans and Ryan was a streetwise brat with too much piss and vinegar running through his veins to even sit down and shut up like he should.

Because of that, Evans had always seen the man as a problem. Even to this day, after Ryan had worked his way up to the rank of detective, Evans seemed to see him as nothing more than a slowly gestating problem, a time bomb that could go off at any minute.

Looks like the minute had come.

"What happened?" Evans said gruffly, looking at a sheet of paper he'd brought in with him.

"I was assaulted," Ryan said flatly, glaring at his boss and seething from the knowledge that the man was very likely enjoying this. "An officer of the law in your county was assaulted, and now he's the one being held in an interrogation room like a common criminal. Do you see a problem with that, Chief?"

Evans's dark eyes slid up from the paper to meet Ryan. They looked him up and down, and, from the gleam in them, Evans found him to be lacking.

"I see a problem, alright," Evans muttered, disgust evident in his voice. "I also see a man who's been in that seat before. So don't act so high and mighty."

Ryan gritted his teeth. While this was far from the first time Evans had thrown his somewhat spotty past in his face, it stung today. Not only was he just doing his job, but all of this seemed stacked against him.

"Whatever you think of me or the things I did when I was a kid, the truth is still the truth," Ryan answered, trying to remain calm. "I'm a detective. I'm *your* detective, and I was assaulted. That's a felony any way you slice it."

"Unless the person who assaulted you thought you were putting an innocent person in danger," Evans said slowly, setting the paper down. "Thomas Kent told me he saw you with hands on his wife."

"She's not his wife," Ryan answered quickly and instinctively. "Not yet, and I would never touch Jillian. I married her, for God's sake."

"Married and divorced," Evans said. "And you're a cop, Devereux. I shouldn't have to tell you how common physical altercations are between married couples, especially married couples where the relationship is strained."

Ryan took a deep breath. If he had ever been this mad in his entire life, he couldn't remember it. Still, he needed to keep his cool about him right now.

"She didn't say that," he said firmly. "We might have had our troubles, but I know Jillian. I would never hit her, and she would never say I did."

Evans blinked at him. "You're right," he finally admitted. "She said her fiancé was wrong. She said she lost her temper and went to strike you. She said you stopped her gently."

"That's exactly what happened," Ryan assured the man, though he was still as mad as hell. "So what's the problem here, Chief?"

Evans slid the piece of paper across the table, staring at Ryan the entire time. "I want you to sign this."

Ryan reached for the paper.

"It's a waiver," Evans said. "Agreeing that you won't take action against Thomas Kent."

"Assaulting a police officer is a felony," Ryan answered. "Even if I didn't want to press charges, there's not much I can do to stop it."

"We're not pressing charges because that's not what happened," Evans said, his eyes narrowing at Ryan. "That man is an op-ed reporter, and I have an alleyway full of people telling me that you and your ex-wife were about to start swinging at each other before he swooped in and broke it up."

"That's not what happened," Ryan barked back.

"While I'm sure that's true, I'm betting the story he'd put in the paper would say otherwise," Evans answered. "You'd lose everything if that sort of rumor came out against you, Ryan. I'm trying to help you."

"That would be a first," Ryan murmured.

"That's your problem, Detective," Evans said. "You think there's only one way to get something done. Coincidentally, that's always your way." He leaned forward in his seat. 'What the hell were you doing following that man?"

"I found a note," Ryan said. "It had information that made me believe he might have had something to do with Haley's murder."

"And you didn't feel the need to share that with your superior officer?" Evans asked.

"It was nothing," Ryan said. "It was a hunch."

"Because," Evans continued, "your superior officer would have told you that you're not the right person to be looking into something like that."

"The hell I'm not," Ryan said. "That man is sleeping a few doors down from my daughter."

"I understand that," Evans said. "But you need to understand that being this close to something can oftentimes lead to sloppy police work, and sloppy police work leads to your being punched in your damn face."

"My face is fine. My face will heal. Haley King won't," Ryan answered.

"Did you know you were a suspect?" Evans said, arching a dark brow at Ryan. "It was my first big case as a freshly-minted detective. We were looking through all the possible leads, and your name came up." He shrugged. "Makes sense. You and Haley had been tight. You were supposed to go to prom together. What if you two had a fight? What if she wouldn't put out and you got pissed about it?"

"That's ridiculous," Ryan answered, his voice shaking a little.

"Yeah," Evans said. "That's what I told them. I said I know that little piss ant. He might have booze on his breath and trouble in his heart, but he is not a killer." He shook his head. "Even back then, I could see something in you. I wasn't sure which way it was going to go. Honestly, sometimes, I'm still not." He nodded at Ryan. "Sign the paper. Then I'll let you talk to Thomas Kent. Just remember, there was a time when someone thought the same thing about you that you're thinking about him."

Ryan scribbled his name on the paper and pushed it back to Evans.

"Good," Evans said, standing up. "And watch the way you conduct yourself. I'm not sure you should have ever been on this case in the first place. Another incident like today and I'm tossing you from it."

Chapter Fourteen

It didn't seem quite fair to Ryan that while he had been made to wait in an interrogation room, Thomas was not only left in the breakroom but also given Jillian to keep him company. When Ryan walked in and caught sight of them holding hands and talking, his heart cracked in a way it hadn't in several months now.

Jillian looked in his direction. "I just want to start by saying I'm sorry," she said. Then, looking over at Thomas, she added, "We both are."

"Great," Ryan muttered, sitting at the table across from the pair.

"How's your lip?" Thomas asked, motioning on his own face at the part of Ryan's that had taken the brunt of the hit.

"Better than you'd think," Ryan said. "Turns out you hit like a girl."

"That's enough," Jillian said, obviously exhausted. "Stop acting like a child."

Ryan's eyes darted to his ex-wife's. "You're the one who just had to apologize. You ever think it might be you who's acting like a child?"

"I overreacted," Jillian admitted. "I shouldn't have, and God knows there's never a good enough reason to resort to violence when arguing. I shouldn't have tried to slap you. I know that, but I wouldn't have been in a position to slap you if you hadn't been following Thomas for no reason."

"You have no idea what reasons I do or don't have, Jillian," Ryan said.

"What is that supposed to mean?" she asked, biting her lower lip.

"It means I was doing my job," he answered.

"Is that all you're going to say?" she asked. "Is that really all you're going to tell me?"

"I don't know how to win with you," Ryan admitted, his voice rising a full octave. "You say I'm too invested in my job. You say I didn't pay you enough attention, and because of that, you went and screwed this idiot." He pointed to Thomas. "And then you left me for him. All because you didn't want to have to hear about my damn job, and now you're pissed because I won't tell you about it. What the hell do you want?"

"I want this to be over," she answered, blinking hard. "I want to know that I don't have to worry about whether or not my daughter's father and the man I'm about to marry are going to make her life a living hell by fighting like kids on a playground."

"If someone is going to make her life hell, it's not going to be me," Ryan answered.

"What are you talking about?" Jillian asked, deflating at the thought of more confrontation.

"I'm talking about him, Jilly. I'm talking about the man you brought into our home, the man you placed in proximity to our little girl. You should have been more careful."

"He was a DJ," Thomas butted in. "She wanted a specific disc jockey for the wedding and I finally convinced him to take the job. I wanted it to be a surprise though. That's what you were watching, Ryan. I was planning the damn wedding."

Ryan looked down and saw Jillian squeeze Thomas's hand. It sent shards of hurt through him.

Still, he clung to what he had. He clung to what he knew. So what if the person he'd seen Thomas paying was some stupid wedding singer or whatever? That had never been what spurred this on in the first place. There had been other evidence, and Ryan was about to lay that out in front of them.

"I know you had something to do with Haley King's murder, Thomas," he said flatly.

"Jesus," Jillian gasped. "Are you serious right now, Ryan? Are you really going to stand there and tell me that you're accusing my fiancé of a twenty-year-old murder because you're mad at him?"

"It's not because I'm mad at him, Jilly," Ryan said. "I couldn't care less about that jackass. It's just that I know what happened. I saw it. I saw the damn letter, Thomas."

"Letter?" Jillian asked. "What letter?"

"A letter he wrote to you," Ryan said. "He called you 'Pookiepie'."

"He always calls me that," she said. Then, with widening eyes, she asked, "You read our love letters? How dare you!"

"The date coincided to when we were still married, so I'm not so sure that you should be the one who feels betrayed about this, Jillian," Ryan said. "But that's neither here nor there, is it, Thomas?"

"What is he talking about?" Jillian asked.

"You're not the first person he's called that," Ryan answered, looking over at Thomas. "You used that same disgusting name with Haley, didn't you?"

"What?" Jillian asked, gasping again. "Thomas?"

Thomas looked at his soon-to-be bride and then at her ex-husband. "We were kids. We were all kids. I didn't say anything because it didn't matter. I didn't want you to think it was a pattern."

"You didn't want me to think what was a pattern?" Jillian asked tepidly.

"When I started seeing Haley, she wasn't single. In fact, she was—"

"You son of a bitch," Ryan said, standing. Ryan's rage went through the roof as he realized what was going on. Not only had this bastard broken up his marriage by sleeping with his wife, but he had also slept with his first girlfriend.

Ryan saw red as he lumbered toward the man. "You're a piece of work, jackass," he said. He didn't even realize what he was doing as his fist pulled back and struck Thomas right in the eye.

The man fell backward, grunting as he slammed onto the floor.

"That," Ryan said, huffing hard, "is how a man punches."

Chapter Fifteen

Feeling as though he were back to square one in terms of his investigation, Detective Devereux decided to head home and get himself a good night's rest. It was a cliché thing to say, but sometimes, it really did help in breaking an investigation. Much like anything else, police work needed time away from it, even if it was only a few hours in bed.

Aromatic sea air billowed up from the water, rising skyward like a tower from the ocean. Ryan Devereux always loved the way the night air smelled as it came in from the sea. To him, it was a smell unlike any other. Fresh, crisp, and salty, the many layers of the water unfolded in a way no perfume could ever hope to mimic. No matter the time of year, the temperature outside, or the how high the waves crashed, the water always smelled the same.

It was the smell of his home, the smell of saltwater mixing with freshwater. The stillness of the marsh as it met the land. South Carolina Lowcountry was a place unlike any other in every way. But in the stillness of the night, it was its unique fragrance that stood out most to Ryan.

Second Wind bobbed slightly in the choppy Atlantic waters that night. Hopefully that, combined with his pure exhaustion, would be enough to help him drift off easily, though somehow, he doubted it.

Stepping off the dock and into his houseboat, Ryan removed his shirt and tossed it on the bed, then made his way to the bathroom. As hot water washed over his tired body, Ryan thought about the last few days, about how much more difficult the already troubled relationship with his ex-wife had gotten. If he was being honest with himself, it wasn't her he was really concerned with. Sure, he still cared for the woman, but she'd made her decision and it seemed she was pretty adamant about sticking with it.

What bothered him the most was the thought that his own troubled relationship may affect his daughter, who at this moment was the most important thing in his life. Knowing that in her home, she was in no direct physical danger was a relief, yes. But that still left the man worried about her emotional state. She was old enough to put the pieces together when her father suddenly stopped showing up for dinner. No longer could he pretend she was a child and that such things would go over her head. Now, he knew better.

"God . . ." he muttered to himself. "I hope she understands how much I love her. How difficult this is for me."

Stepping out of the shower and pulling on a pair of sweatpants, Ryan sat on his bed, then looked over at his dresser. Perched at the end of his bar was the small box given to him by Foggy King, the one he referred to as a 'boyfriend box'. In the drama of the last few days, he hadn't actually taken the time to look inside, but with his nerves running too high to sleep, he figured now was as good a time as any.

The box was about six inches wide and four inches deep, with chipped edges and a bow and arrow embossed in gold paint on its lid. Ryan held it in his hand for a few minutes, looking it over and trying to remember if he'd ever seen it. But try as he might, the damn thing just didn't look familiar.

He opened it. First, he spotted a small porcelain unicorn, one with its foot held outward. It was a small thing, only about four inches wide, but it looked well-made and probably expensive at one time. He picked it up and held it in his hands. It was heavy, with a brightly painted rainbow mane and a metallic gold horn. It reminded him of Haley, not only because he knew it had once belonged to her, but because of how beautiful and delicate she must have found it.

Haley King was always the type to notice the small things, the little bits of character that made things unique and different. She did this no matter where they were, in small cafes, in the woods, on the beach, even noticing Ryan Devereux's eyes. It was true. In his right eye, right there in the middle of the bright blue lay a small brown fleck no bigger than the head of a pin.

She'd noticed it once when they found themselves on the beaches of Sullivan's Island watching the sunrise. Even though Ryan himself had never really noticed the small imperfection, Haley decided right then and there that it was an important part of who he was, the little thing that made him different from any other blue-eyed boy.

She'd even pointed the imperfection out to the young boy's momma, who told him it was just another little something that made him unique. He'd been so embarrassed when they'd sit around the porch late at night talking about him, about how handsome he was, how sweet and kind he was, and how much they both loved him.

Such things made him uncomfortable to no end. Uncle Pauley taught him to be a man's man, that flattery and the like were things only women took part in, which is why any time the two would start down that road, he'd make himself scarce, at least for a little while.

But keeping away from Haley usually proved to be a difficult task. Not twenty minutes would go by before Ryan would inevitably come walking back around the corner with a big smile on his face. He'd grab the young girl's hand and run, laughing all the way until finally getting far enough away from the watchful eyes of his momma to steal a kiss.

He placed the unicorn on the dresser and continued through the box. Trinkets, seven more in all, made up the rest of its contents. Each one was a different type of animal, all porcelain, all similar in size and color. He placed them back in the box, closed it, and lay his head back, hoping the swaying Atlantic waters would lull him to sleep.

But like they say about the best-laid plans . . . Ryan heard a noise coming from the upper deck of his boat. Assuming at first that it was just his Uncle Pauley, he turned to his side and closed his eyes again.

A loud crash soon followed, echoing down the stairs and into his bedroom. He leapt to his feet, grabbed his gun, slid on a pair of sneakers, and made his way up the stairs. Just as his head rose up from the bottom level, a shot rang out in his direction. A bullet zoomed by, narrowly missing his head and busting through the fiberglass railing of his boat.

"Hold it. Charleston Police!" he yelled, then popped his head up.

In the far corner, his uncle Pauley lay wounded, blood puddling under him. Ryan quickly shot a couple of rounds toward the hooded figure standing next to his uncle. Then, like a flash, the man was gone, leaving Pauley wounded on the floor of his nephew's houseboat.

"Pauley!" Ryan cried out, running to his side.

"He shot me . . ." Pauley said.

Careful not to move him too much, Ryan searched for the entry wound, running his hands around his uncle's chest and neck until finally finding it near his right shoulder. "I think it's a flesh wound," Ryan said, instinctively reaching for his phone and realizing it wasn't there. "Hold on! I'm going to call someone!"

Even though his training told him it was only a flesh wound and that his uncle would be okay, he still couldn't stop his mind and heart from racing. Pauley had been a part of his life for so long that the thought of not having him around now seemed almost too much to bear.

Detective Devereux ran back downstairs, then to his surprise he was greeted with another round of bullets firing toward him. Quickly diving to the floor and taking cover behind his bed, Ryan fired off a shot of his own, striking the man through the leg. Yelling out in pain, the figure quickly headed out the rear door of Ryan's boat and up the stairs, vanishing into the darkness.

Grabbing his phone and dialing help, the detective noticed something odd. The small box on his dresser seemed to have been rifled through. On the floor just below the dresser lay the small unicorn statue, its leg chipped and its horn broken clean off. Aside from that, there seemed to be a few things missing.

What he was sure he'd counted as eight small porcelain trinkets were now only four.

"911, what is your emergency?" the operator said.

Chapter Sixteen

"How you feeling?" Ryan asked, stepping into his uncle's room at Roper St. Francis Hospital.

He'd been there a few times over the last year after meeting one of the nurses while strolling Market Street. She was a pretty thing with sandy blonde hair, brown eyes, and a sweet little smile. Their first night out, she took him wine tasting, which, if he was being honest, wasn't his favorite thing in the world. But they'd managed to hit it off well enough to go out a few more times before Ryan had decided to end things.

She was a great girl, sure. But he couldn't help but get the feeling she was looking for something a little more serious than he was ready for at the moment. In the beginning, he wasn't sure he'd remember which floor she worked, but after stepping off the elevator, he realized it was the same one his uncle was on.

Due to years of working and drinking in the southern heat, Pauley wasn't in the best physical condition, so to assume he'd be spending the next few days in the hospital seemed like a pretty fair bet. Which is why the detective doubted he'd make it through that much time without running across Michelle at least once.

"Oh, yeah," Pauley said, coughing and hacking as though he were trying to get up a furball. "I'm feeling just fine."

He wasn't sure if the man was serious or trying to be coy. Either way, the truth was written all over him. Pauley Wells was once a beast of a man, strong and loud, with enough energy to put that little pink bunny from the commercials to shame. But now, after all these Lowcountry years, he was a different person. A weaker person.

"You need to start taking care of yourself," Ryan said, sitting on the chair beside his uncle. "Otherwise, you won't be around much longer."

"I'm strong." Pauley smiled. "I'll make it."

"Everyone makes it until they don't," Ryan replied. "You're alive until you're not. After that . . . you're just gone. You need to start taking care of yourself."

"Tell me there, Sonny," his uncle said, tugging at the wires taped to his chest. "Were you on television this morning punching out your wife, or was that the morphine I was seeing?"

"No," Ryan answered. "That was me. Though I wasn't punching my ex-wife."

"No," her unmistakable voice spoke from behind him. "It was actually the other way around."

"Well . . ." Pauley struggled, trying his best to sit up. "Look what the waves washed in. Hello, pretty lady." He smiled, extending his arms and hugging Jillian.

"Pauley." She smiled, wrapping her arms around him.

"We brought you something," Carly said, holding up a gift bag.

Maybe it was because her own family was such a mess, or maybe the two just naturally clicked. But for whatever reason, Pauley and Jillian had always seemed to think the world of one another, still speaking every week even though she was no longer married to his nephew. But isn't that 'too friendly to be mean' attitude just like a Southern girl?

"Really?" Pauley put on a wide-eyed smile. "What is it?" He tore through the bag like a mole through a garden. "Hey . . . sunglasses."

"I picked them myself." Carly grinned. "Do you like them?"

"I love them," he said, hugging her tightly.

In all the years he'd known his uncle, Ryan Devereux had never once seen him wear or heard him mention sunglasses. And he doubted this was the day that would change. But he knew how to be nice, how to accept a gift for the thought and nothing else. It was that thoughtful attitude that provided a shoulder for Jillian to lean on through those early days of Ryan's marriage to her.

Leaning back against the wall and watching the way his uncle spoke to his wife and daughter made Ryan miss the days when that sort of thing was ordinary. They rambled on for what seemed like an hour, talking about everything but which way the wind was blowing.

From the corner of his eye, he noticed a figure standing in the doorway, staring at him. Feeling almost unnerved for a moment, he turned to see Michelle Myers, the spritely nurse he'd dated a few months before. A crooked grin rested on her face as her eyes glimmered with something close to excitement.

"Excuse me for a moment," he muttered, though not loud enough to actually draw any looks.

"Long time no see," Michelle said as he stepped into the hallway.

"Yeah . . ." Ryan answered. "I've been kind of busy with everything. You know?"

"I saw you on the news this morning." She folded her arms across her chest. "I wouldn't have taken you for the streetfighter type."

"It was just a misunderstanding. A simple misunderstanding . . ."

Only since standing this close to her did Ryan realize how much he missed this. It wasn't so much the girl. Sure, she was sweet, cute, and everything any guy would love. What he missed was having someone to talk to, someone he shared a spark with, the kind that you feel in conversation. The kind that's evident even for onlookers.

"How are things going with you?" she asked. "Dating anyone?"

"No," he answered. "What about you?"

"Once upon a time . . ." She ran a hand through her hair. "But he moved away. Now, I'm all alone. Footloose and fancy free."

"Really?" Ryan answered. "Good to know."

There was a part of him that wanted to reach out and grab the girl, to hold her in his arms and ask her out. But he didn't. He held back. It wouldn't be fair to her to ask her to come back to a relationship he wasn't sure had any future. It was obvious to Ryan that he was ready to move on, but it was just much less obvious with whom he wanted to do it.

"That's me." She pointed to a small speaker on the ceiling.

A series of three soft dings rang out through the long white hallway. Michelle turned on her heels and with a big smile walked back toward the reception desk.

"She's cute," Jillian said from behind him.

He turned to see his ex-wife leaned against the doorframe. He wondered how long she'd been standing there and how much she'd heard. Did he sound like an idiot, like a hot-to-trot adolescent looking for his first hookup? Lord, he hoped not. Though in truth, that would be one of the lesser embarrassing things Jillian had seen him do over the years.

"Yeah," he answered. "She's a sweet girl. But I'm actually glad you came. I wanted to talk to you about something."

"Oh, yeah?" Jillian asked. "And what's that?"

"I need you to leave," he replied, shuffling his feet just a little. "I want you to get out of Charleston for a little while."

"Ryan," she said, rolling her head back a little. "Is that really necess—"

"Yes," he interrupted. "It really is. Lord willing and the creek don't rise, these threats won't amount to anything, but just in case, just on the off chance whoever is behind this tries to hurt me . . . I can't risk having Carly caught up in that. I can't risk either of you."

"I appreciate that. I really do," she responded. "But I think we'll be okay."

"Hopefully." He stepped closer to her. "But you can only be wrong about that once. I need you to be right about it every day. And right now, the best chance of that happening is for you to leave Lowcountry."

The words cut into him more than he thought they would. Yes, sending his daughter away was the wise thing to do, but that didn't mean it was an easy thing to do. Watching his little girl walk away would tear at his heart in a way nothing else ever had. He knew that, and while he was sure he wasn't ready for the pain, he knew what needed to be done.

"Can I talk to you?" he asked, pulling Carly aside.

"What's wrong?"

"Nothing," he answered, wrapping his hands around her thin upper arms. "You and your mom are gonna go on a little trip. I need you to promise me that you'll listen to her. That you'll do what she asks and stay by her side."

"Dad." Carly's eyes began to flood with tears. "What's going on?"

"I need you to promise me Carly," he repeated, "that you'll do as she says. Can you promise me that?"

"Dad, please."

"Carly," he said, pulling her closer. "Can you do it? Can you say the words?"

"I . . . I promise," she said, her head falling into his chest.

Her hot breath pushed through his cotton shirt as she dug her face deeper into his chest. The young girl was afraid, that was obvious. But so was her father. The thought of her not being in the same city was almost enough to make him pull back on his request, but he knew better than to let emotion govern him in this moment, never mind the emotional tug-of-war going on inside him. The safety of his family was paramount.

"Go." He looked to Jillian. "Pack a few things. Head out of town."

Chapter Seventeen

"What are you doing here?" Ryan asked, seeing his partner sitting on the deck of his houseboat.

"How's your uncle?" she asked, dodging his question.

"He was shot," Ryan answered, stopping on the edge of the dock. "So, not too great. Again, what are you doing here?"

"I'm not welcome?" she raised an eyebrow.

"Kit . . ."

"Fine," she answered after a long silence. "Someone broke into your boat."

"What? Who? How do you know?"

"We received a call," she said, "from someone who just happened to see a man with a ski-mask and a flashlight poking around your boat."

"Why did no one call me?" he asked, wiping a blanket of sweat from his neck.

"Chief said not to," Kit answered. "It was your night off. Besides . . . I think maybe he thought you'd overreact."

"Did you catch the guy?"

"Nope. By the time we got here, he was gone. Left nothing but a footprint."

"A footprint?" Ryan raised an eyebrow. "Where?"

"Just outside your bedroom," she replied. "Its still wet, and since you've been out all day, I figure it had to come from whoever broke in. That, and it was a Sketchers sneaker. I didn't see any in your closet."

"Nope," Ryan said, looking at the print. "I don't own a pair of Sketchers. Besides, this print has the Georgia Tech logo on them. At least that's what it looks like."

"Is that what that is?" Kit asked, kneeling down and getting a closer look at the dirty footprint.

There was something in Kit's movements, a reservation that let him know she wanted to say something but she still hadn't found the right way, and the detective was pretty sure he knew what that something was. "Spit it out," he said.

"I just don't want you to lose your job over this."

"If I lose my job for doing my job, then the damn thing ain't worth having anyhow," he snapped, marching past Kit into his bedroom. "Now you've got a problem too?" he said, pulling his shirt over his head and tossing it to the bed. "Just tell me, Kit. Tell me whatever it is you're trying not to say."

"You're too close to this," she said. "It's blinding you. This is a conflict of interest and you know it. You may be doing more harm than good—"

"More harm than good? I can't believe you're saying this to me. Any good detective cares about the job they do. You should try it sometime!"

"Hey." A pang of anger rose in his partner's voice. "I care about what I do. I just know how to keep my emotions in check, that's all. Or maybe punching people out and accusing everyone under the sun of crimes they didn't commit is the mark of a good detective."

"Why are you here?" he asked.

"To make sure you don't end up doing something stupid."

"Did the chief *send* you here?" Ryan asked, his breath slowing. "To watch me?"

"He may have suggested I spend a little time with you," Kit replied. "Which I'm now beginning to regret doing."

"Great," Ryan replied, turning his back to her. "Then just go. I won't overreact. I won't chase down any leads. I won't do anything. I'll spend the rest of the night here. Then, come morning, I'll start again."

"Ryan," she said, stepping closer to him and placing her hand on his bare shoulder.

It was the first time since becoming his partner that she'd ever touched him. Her hands were soft and warm, comforting in a way he hadn't expected from a cop. An easy warmth radiated from her body, cascading down his chest then melting into his skin. He felt her step closer, her body next to his as she leaned in.

"I'm just asking you to take it slow," she said, removing her hand and heading for the door.

"I can take it slow," he answered. "But I can't stop. I'm going to do my job regardless of what anyone says or thinks. If you can't get onboard with that, then maybe you should find a new partner."

"I don't want a new partner," she answered. "I like the one I have. Now come on. Let's search this boat. Maybe I missed something the first time around."

They were both strong-willed and forthright, and the relationship between the two had always seemed pretty straightforward. That is, until tonight. It's strange how one little conversation can change the dynamic of two people in such a profound way. He'd never thought of his partner as someone who might think he couldn't handle himself under the stress of the job, and he'd certainly never thought of her as . . . as a woman.

"Fine," Ryan answered, sliding a faded Chevrolet T-shirt over his head and heading to the deck.

"See anything out of the ordinary?" Kit asked.

"No. Not yet, anyway."

For the most part, everything seemed pretty much the way he'd left it, with only a few Corona cans toppled over, likely the work of the cool Atlantic winds. In addition to this being the first time he'd felt her touch, it also marked one of the very few times he'd seen the woman in anything other than pants.

A pair of light denim shorts wrapped her thin frame and a dark green t-shirt clung to her body. Small streaks of sweat could be seen through the shirt, running down her back and around her neck. But living his entire life in Lowcountry, Ryan knew it only took a few seconds in the Carolina heat for your body to begin dripping like a faucet.

"How was the movie?" Kit asked, kneeling down.

"What movie?" Ryan replied.

"Some like it hot . . ." She smiled, holding out a small sliver of paper.

"What are you talking about?"

"Some like it hot," she repeated. "You went to the revival showing at the new theater."

"No, I didn't," Ryan said. "I've never seen that movie in my life."

"Well, someone did," she said, handing Ryan a movie stub. "See . . . some like it hot. One o'clock today."

"Well, it wasn't me," Ryan said. "And it wasn't Pauley. He's in the hospital."

"You know what this means." She stepped closer, taking the ticket from his hand. "It could have only come from whoever broke in. They must have dropped it."

"What the hell kind of person goes to see a Marilyn Monroe movie, then breaks into my house?"

Kit's eyes narrowed. "That's what we need to figure out."

"We?"

She looked to him, her lips parting like she wanted to say something. There were a million things Ryan wanted to say too. He just couldn't find the right words at the moment. Though, the longer she stood there, it seemed like his partner couldn't either. They were two in the same, strong-willed and determined not to let anything hamper what they were trying to do, and as the night faded further into the morning, it seemed as though they were beginning to realize that.

Chapter Eighteen

Parked outside Kit's house, Ryan waited for her to get dressed. The morning sun was hot, filling the air with a blanket of thick, sizzling stickiness. After finding the movie stub in the houseboat, the two partners decided to go check the place out. He wasn't sure what they'd find or even what they were looking for aside from maybe some surveillance video, but they had to check it out.

With his wife and daughter out of town, his uncle in the hospital, and the chief of police breathing down his throat about this investigation, he knew he needed to move carefully. There had already been too much commotion around this cold case and he didn't need any more eyes turned on him.

Kit's house sat just at the edge of Sullivan's Island. She bought it on a whim after moving to Lowcountry, not even realizing the real estate potential of the place. Sullivan's Island was a gorgeous place, with sweeping ocean views, an old-world feel, and all the charm South Carolina had to offer. She seemed to like the place well enough, though Ryan wasn't sure she appreciated it for everything it was worth.

"Hey," she said, opening the door of his car and getting in. Her hair sat high atop her head in a tight ponytail, a style she'd spent the first few months of her time in Charleston refusing to wear. But with the arrival of one-hundred-and-one-degree summer days and full humidity, she'd quickly changed her tune.

"Hey. Sleep well?"

"Well enough, I guess," she replied, her voice still a bit unsteady from the early morning hour.

The drive into town was a slow one. Without much traffic to deal with, getting around the friendly city was usually a relatively pain-free experience. Though today, his car seemed to somehow move even slower than it usually did.

The two partners had spent much of the night before sitting on the upper deck of Ryan's houseboat, sometimes discussing the things that brought them to where they were. Other times, they'd just sit for a while, silently watching the waves ripple across the water.

Ryan Devereux always found something special and almost magical about slow nights on the southern shore. Watching the water and sharing a few drinks always seemed to help things make sense. It was as though the truth that hid in the Carolina heat just disappeared with the setting sun, replaced by a feeling of safety that blew in along with the night breeze.

"Feeling better?" Kit looked to her partner. "After some sleep, I mean?"

"Yeah." Ryan turned down Eighth Street. "I've just had a lot on my mind lately."

At the corner of Eighth Street sat what during the days of his childhood was a pharmacy but now was a small dress boutique. Every time he passed by those big glass doors, the same memory invaded his mind. It brought him back to his childhood with Haley King.

Ryan and Haley would spend each Christmas weekend acting out one of the most famous scenes in all of American film history. He would pretend to work behind the small soda fountain, she'd place her order, and they would talk about their dreams, each time with him insisting she get coconut on her sundae just as they'd seen so many times on his momma's worn-out copy of *It's a Wonderful Life*.

"What are you thinking about?" Kit asked, noticing the distance in his eyes.

"Haley," he answered before even realizing he'd spoken. "She loved that old pharmacy."

"What pharmacy?"

"That dress shop . . ." Ryan replied. "It used to be a pharmacy. It had a little soda fountain too."

History is a strange thing, making up our memories yet somehow managing to change little bits with each new sunset. It was almost as though just because someone wanted their lives to seem a little happier in their mind, they could rewrite time. He'd lived in the South his whole life, seeing each Christmas come and go with the mild Lowcountry winter. Yet, in his memories, Haley was standing in the snow-covered Charleston streets.

"Here we are," Ryan said, pulling into the movie theater's parking lot.

The Charleston County Fifteen was a rather new place, having been built just across the street from the old Confederate Seven. They'd originally planned to tear down the old place, but after a ton of backlash and an entire county filled with history-loving Southerners, Charleston County decided to declare the thing a historical landmark, thereby saving the old building and the tons of memories it housed.

"Excuse me . . ." Ryan said, walking through the small side door.

Near the concession stand stood an older gentleman with a thick silver beard and a shiny bald head. Ryan recognized him as Jacob Cyrus. Some years back, the two men were involved in what you might call a small land dispute after Ryan's momma died and

Mr. Cyrus decided the fact that she owed him a bit of money entitled him to a piece of her property. In the end, the two men had managed to settle their differences, though they hadn't had much to do with one another since. That was going to have to change now, though, because as Jacob Cyrus was the manager of this particular cinema, Ryan was about to have to ask him for a favor.

"I need to see your security tapes," Ryan said.

"Detective Devereux," Jacob said, not looking up from the stack of papers he was reading. "Now why would you want to see my tapes?"

"It's part of an investigation."

"Would this be the same investigation that caused you to punch your ex-wife's fiancé in the street?" He smiled.

"I can get a warrant if I have to," he said, knowing the chances of that actually happening were pretty doubtful. "I just need last night's showing of *'Some like it hot'.*"

"That actually went better than I thought it would," Mr. Cyrus said, scratching his head with a pen. "Quite a nice turnout for that one."

His tactics were amateur. The whole *not looking up because you're not important enough* thing was old-hat. Ryan had seen it a million times over. He'd also seen it done much better by people with far more experience at manipulating the emotions of those around them—in other words, cops and criminals.

"What about it?" Ryan asked, stepping close enough to invade the man's personal space.

"Sorry. No can do. The footage isn't saved. It goes onto some kind of hard drive, then once the drive is full, it rewrites unless we stop it."

"This was yesterday's footage," Ryan replied. "How often does it rewrite?"

"Every morning." He looked up at the detective. "Looks like you just missed the cut." The petty pleasure in his voice was enough to make Ryan's stomach turn. How anyone could get off on such small inconveniences only spoke to how truly weak the man was.

Kit stepped forward. "Which theater was last night's showing held in?"

"Eight," the manager said, somehow looking at her with even more disdain than he used to look at Ryan.

"I assume we're free to go look around?" Kit asked, throwing a bucket's worth of disapproval in his face. "Unless, of course, you have a problem?"

"No problem," Jacob answered. "Why don't you head on down the hall? Fourth door on your right. I'll go bring up the lights."

"Great," Ryan replied as he and Kit headed down the long hallway.

Like most new movie theaters, the place was piped in bright lights that pulsated an array of ever-changing neon colors. Old movie posters lined the walls featuring everything from *The Ten Commandments* to *Citizen Kane*. Phrases like *IMAX* and *GTX* glowed brightly all around the room, calling out from every dark corner.

"This looks more like a dance club than a movie theater, doesn't it?" Ryan asked his partner.

"Please." Kit sighed. "You should see the damn theaters where I'm from. I'm surprised someone hasn't gone into an epileptic fit just walking through the hallway. It's sad that this kind of crap draws people in. Doesn't speak well for the movies themselves, does it?"

If there was one constant about his partner, it was that she always spoke her mind and was never at a loss for words. He'd been in an array of situations with her and never once had she held back or not known what to say.

"That's subtle," Kit said, stepping through the doorway and into theater eight.

Lowcountry pride! said the huge glittering letters hanging on both sides of the seats.

Yes, Southerners were proud people, but Ryan Devereux knew for a fact it wasn't a movie theater that made them that way. The South he'd been raised in, the one he'd come to love and appreciate so much, ran through with country girls and backroad boys, each one as proud as a peacock of the mud on their tires and the sweat on their backs.

Sure, everyone went to the movies once in a while, but in Lowcountry, it was backyard barbeques and beachside bonfires that people looked forward to, not whatever nonsense Tom Cruise was spouting at the moment.

"Excuse me," Kit said, approaching a young man.

Daniel, according to the tag on his shirt. He looked to be about seventeen or eighteen years old with dark curly hair and big button eyes. In his hand was a broom and dustpan, and hanging from his mouth was a half-eaten piece of licorice. Classy.

"I'm detective Walker, and this is my partner, Detective Devereux. We'd like to ask you a few questions about last night." Kit flashed her badge.

"Last night?" he repeated, his lip beginning to quiver just a little.

"Yes," Ryan answered, noticing him pull his sleeves down in an attempt to hide a few scratches on his arm. "Last night."

There was a nervous energy to him, to the way he moved and carried himself. To seasoned detectives like the two standing across from him, he looked like the kind of guy you see on the street that runs at the sight of a police car, likely because of what they're hiding in the pockets of their oversized jeans.

Ryan noticed his shoes. "Sketchers. Georgia Tech Sketchers."

The sound of the young man's metal-handled broom crashing against the floor echoed across the theater as his eyes suddenly grew wide, and he made a beeline for the back door. Springing into action, the two detectives chased after him, through the door and onto the street.

"You go that way!" Ryan said, pointing to the left.

Ryan turned to his right, running around the side of the theater, where he spotted the young man about one hundred feet ahead of him. Sprinting faster, he began to gain on him as they ran toward Magnolia Road.

Turning to see Ryan gaining on him, the boy made a quick turn, leaping over a row of bushes and into the street, where he collided with an oncoming car. Ryan watched as his body jetted forward, bouncing down the busy street before skidding to a stop near the curb.

"Shit!" Ryan yelled, running full-speed toward him.

Chapter Nineteen

The young man turned out to be Billy Edwards, the son of a local fisherman whose record appeared to be pretty clean. Ryan tried not to stare at the cuts and scrapes covering his arms and face. Not appearing to weigh more than a hundred and ten pounds or so, it wasn't hard to see how he'd sustained so much bodily damage from the impact.

A pang of guilt ran through the detective's body as he looked down at the young man from his bedside. Even though he knew a suspect's running away wasn't his fault, nor was what danger they found themselves in after doing it, he still couldn't help but shake the feeling that if he hadn't been there questioning him, the boy would likely be at work right now.

Being a detective never seemed to get any easier, though. There was the compassionate side to things, sure. But there was also the flip side of it all. This man likely broke into his home, riffled through his things, and perhaps even shot his uncle. Should the fact that he was young alleviate all of his wrongdoing? What about the other side of that? What if going easy on this guy would only allow him to go out and commit other crimes?

Chief Evans entered the room. "He's lucky to be alive."

A potent mix of anger and frustration dripped from him with such intensity that Ryan could almost see it pooling under his feet. His arms were folded behind his back and his gait made the man almost appear to be moving in slow-motion as he circled Billy's bed, keeping his lips pursed and his eyes focused on the victim.

Dramatic to a fault, Chief Evans made sure to let you know exactly what he was thinking at all times in spectacular fashion. Overexaggerated facial expressions, lingering looks, and a southern drawl so thick it could sink a ship suddenly emerged each time he tried to stress a point. Today was no exception.

"Nineteen years old," the chief said. "And now he's lying in a hospital bed pumped full of drugs."

"This wasn't my fault," Ryan answered. "I was questioning—"

"I've heard," he interrupted, adding a few extra syllables to his words. "You were questioning him and he ran."

"Right."

"Then you chased him into traffic."

Not the type of guy to beat around the bush, Chief Evans got right to the point, throwing blame toward Ryan with enough humidity-fueled anger that he knew he was in for a world of talking to. He also knew nothing he said would quell the chief's desire to make him out to be the villain here.

"He leapt over a line of bushes," Ryan clarified. "I was a hundred feet away."

"A hundred feet away but headed in his direction."

"What do you want me to say?" Ryan asked. "I know it looks bad, but I was doing my job."

"Why were you there? Why question him?"

"My house was broken into last night," Ryan answered.

"You mean that boat?" he scoffed, flicking a small bit of what Ryan chose to believe was Spanish moss from his shirt.

"It's a houseboat," Ryan replied. "And I like it. Someone was there snooping around, which marks the second time my home has been broken into. Whoever did it left behind a shoeprint and a movie ticket. When I went there, I saw Billy wearing the same shoes. I asked him about it and that's when he bolted."

Chief Evans raised his eyes, focusing on Ryan. He could almost feel the heat of his stare as his superior searched his mind for the right words. Much like the Spanish moss hanging from every tree in Charleston County, Chief Evans had a history in this town, one he was willing to protect at any cost, and with one of his detectives suddenly popping up on the news for assault then damn-near chasing a young man to his death, it was no big assumption to think he was getting ready to do something drastic.

Ryan expected a long, drawn-out conversation, one that led to a discussion so heated one of them would storm out, nearly taking the door off its hinges as they slammed it. It had happened at least a dozen times before. But there was something different about this time. The chief seemed to have himself more together, calmer and more collected than any other time they'd spoken, and that scared Ryan a little bit.

Surely, he wasn't about to do the unthinkable. Surely, he wasn't going to play the one card Ryan couldn't overcome, right? Seeing his breathing slow and his pupils dilate, Ryan watched intently as the chief's lips parted. "I'm taking you off the case," he said flatly.

"You can't do that," Ryan replied, feeling a pang of something sharp run through his body.

"I can, and I will." The chief turned his gaze out the seventh-story window.

Charleston County stretched out around them in every direction. It was Ryan's home and one of the truest parts of his soul. Seeing the bright orange sun melt into the Atlantic made his heart flutter every time, and this was no exception. So how was it that he'd managed to find himself in a place where he felt alone, alienated in a place so familiar?

"So that's it, then? You hand me a case and tell me to solve it. Then when I try, you reprimand me?"

"She was killed twenty years ago, Devereux," the chief said. "Who's to say the killer is still around? Maybe they were passing through. Maybe they died too."

"No," Ryan said. "Whoever murdered Haley is still here. I know it. That girl was as timid as a newborn buck. She wouldn't have gone off with just anyone. This is someone we know."

"You don't know that. Besides, this is a cold case, Detective," the chief answered. "You're supposed to be behind a desk, looking through papers, studying maps and old interview recordings. You're not supposed to be running around my city causing so much chaos. These cases are based on history. You study history in books."

His words sliced through the detective like a knife, cutting him deeply enough that he was sure he'd feel it for days. How could anyone raised in Charleston say those words? How could the chief of police not see what the rest of the world knew to be true?

"History," Ryan snapped. "This is Charleston. This is Lowcountry. History is in our blood, Chief. It's what we're made of. The people in this town . . . they've been here for generations. Haley King means something here. She's just as much a part of this city as anything else."

"It doesn't matter—"

"It does matter," Ryan said. "Haley matters. She mattered then and she matters now, just like every other person in this place. This city spent twenty years missing a piece of itself, a part of its history. If I can bring that back, if I can find that missing piece, then I'm damn sure gonna do it."

"You won't," he answered, turning back to Ryan. "You're off the case. That's it."

"I'll continue the search on my own."

"Do that . . . and you're off the force." The chief exited the room.

He wanted to reach out and grab him, to take his boss by the arm and explain all the reasons he was wrong for doing what he was doing. But that wouldn't do anyone any good and he knew it. But how could he just sit there and leave a murderer free to wander the streets of his hometown?

Chapter Twenty

Ryan hadn't left *Second Wind* in two days when he received a visit from his partner. It seemed no matter what he did, no matter how many hours he spent staring out at the endless Atlantic sky, he couldn't get his anger to subside.

The thought that this person was out there was enough to drive him crazy. More than that, though, was the thought that once again, Haley King would be forgotten. Her body, like her memory, would be swept under the rug. Just like in high school, he would have failed her. Ryan couldn't let that happen. He couldn't just sit around and twiddle his thumbs, even if that meant losing his job.

"How's it going?" Kit asked. She looked fresh and rested, a stark contrast from the mess of anger, paranoia, and self-neglect that Ryan was at the moment.

"Kinda pissed, still. What about you?"

"I'm handling it," she said. "I finally managed to convince the chief I'd been here long enough that I didn't need a partner."

"You're solo?"

"Like Han himself. Though, only until you're ready to come back." She smiled. "I just wanted to stop by and see if you needed anything."

"You giving out assignments?" he asked. "I could use something to fill this time."

"Evans said you'd be back in a day or two."

"Right . . ." he replied. "Just not on my case."

Kit took a seat next to him, leaning forward and staring out at the crystal water. He still remembered the first time they'd met, when she'd told him she didn't really like the water. He wondered how anyone could make such a statement, how anyone could not hear the siren song of the cool Atlantic waters and the hot Carolina nights.

But Kit wasn't Southern, not at heart, anyway. To truly be Southern, you just have to be born here. People below the Mason-Dixon line were God-fearing, kind, strong, and resilient. And while a lot of people from other places might be able to say that same thing, they weren't able to say it with a true Southern drawl, the kind that lingers long after the words have left your lips and the sweat has left your skin.

That's not to say he didn't think a lot of his partner. He did. After all, each time they went out together, his life was in her hands and hers in his. That kind of thing builds trust and appreciation no matter where you're from.

"Is that such a bad thing?" she asked.

"What is that supposed to mean?" Ryan asked with flared nostrils.

Kit sighed. "Maybe it's for the best."

"What are you saying?"

"I'm saying . . . maybe the chief is right. Maybe you could use some time away from the case."

"How can you say that?" Ryan asked. "You know what this case means to me. It's what made me want to be a damn cop in the first place. It was supposed to be me. I was supposed to be with her that night. When they told me she hadn't shown up for the prom, I did nothing. I just sat in my room, stewing in my anger. Do you have any idea what that's like?"

"Yes," Kit said. "I do."

"What?"

"Back home, before I came to South Carolina, I got this call one night. My shift had just ended and I was heading up the stairs." Kit sighed, her voice beginning to slow. "I recognized the address. It was only a few blocks away, but I was tired. I stood there for a second, trying to convince myself to turn around and head down there, but then another car picked up the call. So I just went home."

You can hear it when people's voices fill with regret. It's like a weight is pressing against their throat, as if it's trying to close in on them. I recognized it from interviews, from the wives who just snapped, the friends who'd let jealousy and greed overtake them. People had different ways of dealing with mistakes, but most only had one way of talking about them.

"He was young, a beat-cop. The thing went bad, probably because he didn't know what the hell he was doing out there yet, and he was shot. He didn't make it. It wasn't long after that when I decided to leave town." Kit took a slow, heavy breath.

Ryan had never really put much thought into what his partner's life was like before she came to Lowcountry. She'd never been the type to offer up much in the way of personal information, which made this reveal all the more intriguing, though it did little to quell his own feelings of guilt and regret.

"I'm sorry," Ryan said. "I get how hard that must be for you. I'd tell you that it wasn't your fault, and I'd be right. It wouldn't matter, though, would it? You'd replay it over and over again. You'd let it drive you, assuming it didn't destroy you. That's why I can't just sit here. I have to do something. I have to go out there. Surely, you get that."

"I get it," she answered, walking to the edge of the deck. "I really do, but I've also seen the way these things tear people up. I've seen cops get hung up on a specific case and I've watched what happens after. I know she meant a lot to you, but you can't let this be your undoing. She wouldn't want that."

"She wouldn't want anything. Can't want anything when you're in the ground. And it's not about what she meant to me." Ryan watched his partner stare out into the endless Lowcountry night. "It's about Charleston. It's about every one of us. It's not fair for her to just be forgotten. Not in a town that prides itself on history and good people."

"Everyone gets forgotten sooner or later, Ryan. That's the way of the world, and regardless of how much you might want to, you can't save the world."

"I know that," Ryan answered. "I couldn't even save her. I have to try though. I have to at least try to make it right."

She turned back, keeping her eyes focused on Ryan. Under the bright white moon of the South Carolina sky, she looked a little softer, a little less severe and put-together than she always seemed during their days together. She'd let her guard down, shown herself as vulnerable in a way she hadn't before. Ryan couldn't help but stare a beat too long.

She wasn't wearing a silky white beach dress that hung to the floor. Her long hair wasn't blowing in the breeze, and he couldn't smell any perfume wafting through the air. None of the standard clichés seemed to fit the woman. But what he did see was someone he realized he wanted to know better. And in another light . . .

"I'm not going to be able to stop you, am I?" she asked.

"You know me well enough that I don't need to answer that question. I made a vow to figure out what happened to her, and I'm going to stick to it, whatever the cost."

"Then promise me this." She stepped closer. "That you'll be safe, and that the second you find anything at all, you call me. We'll tell the chief it was me, that I was working the case."

"That's kind of you," he said, "but I can't say I'm too concerned with what the chief thinks right now."

"I'm concerned," she said. "About you. So promise me."

"Fine," he said, nodding at her. "I promise."

"Good," she said, smiling as brightly as the moon. "Now go take a shower. You're starting to smell like a sailor."

Chapter Twenty-One

Ryan spent the better part of his morning tailing Billy Edwards as he bounced around downtown Charleston as though he were a buoy in a storm. Watching him from the shadows, Ryan was reminded of his own youth in Lowcountry and how he and his friends would do the same things he now watched this young man do.

Whether it was spending the day on the beach or in Waterfront Park, there just always seemed to be something to do in his treasured city, a trend which continued well into the detective's adulthood. With its rich cultural flavor, complex history, and seemingly endless restaurants, bars, and shops, getting bored in Charleston wasn't really an option.

For a while, it went pretty uneventfully, with Billy making a few small stops by various businesses, mostly just chatting up the employees before moving on down the line. But as the humidity began to rise and the sweat began to pour, it seemed young Billy's idea of what his day was going to look like changed a bit.

Coming to a sudden stop near the end of an alley behind a small seafood restaurant, Billy did the strangest thing. Ryan's eyes widened as he watched the young man pick up a garbage bag—the only one with a red tag—hoist it over his back, and head off down the street.

"What the hell . . ." he muttered to himself, watching Billy skate out of the alley, toss his skateboard into the back of a small truck, then hop in the driver's seat and head down Palmetto Street.

Ryan wasn't sure what was in the bag, but he knew it wasn't garbage. Maybe once in a lifetime, if even then . . . that's about how often someone grabbed a random garbage bag from the street and took it with them. At least now, his meandering around town for nearly two hours made sense. Young Billy must have been waiting on the drop. The bag must have been planned.

Wanting to see what was in the bag, Ryan thought about Kit's words to him. *The second you find anything at all, call me.* Keeping a tail on the young man, Ryan reached for his phone, but just as he slid his hand across the screen, an opportunity presented itself. It seemed Billy needed a few provisions as he turned into a small gas station on the edge of town.

"Good a time as any . . ." Ryan turned in, then parked a few spaces over.

Once the young man was inside, Ryan hopped out of his car and made his way to Billy's truck faster than a greyhound. The windows were down, probably due to the fact that the truck didn't look to have air conditioning and it was over a hundred degrees outside. Whatever the reason, though, Ryan was happy he wouldn't have to waste any time trying to pick a lock.

Reaching his arm into the small brown vehicle and tugging at the bag, he found it heavier than it looked to be. But the bigger surprise came when he managed to get a peek of its contents. In the small bag were at least six stacks of cold-hard cash and a bottle of red wine. Though Ryan was more of a beer guy, he noticed the fancy label on the bottle, studded with French writing.

Something pinged at the back of his mind. He had seen this bottle before. He had seen this French writing, and he knew exactly where. It had been sitting on a shelf in Foggy's house the last time he was there.

Something clicked, suddenly seeming to make sense. If this boy had been roping around in his houseboat looking for something, and Ryan was certain that he was, then Foggy's insistence on keeping his sister's case closed could have been for a different reason than just wanting to keep the past in the past.

Foggy might have been involved in this after all. Foggy might have had something to do with his sister's murder twenty years ago.

Looking up from the bag, Ryan saw the boy at the register. He had a soda bottle and a pack of cigarettes.

"Lunch of champions," Ryan muttered. He wanted nothing more than to slap this guy around. After all, he had gravely injured his uncle. He couldn't do that though. He was finally getting somewhere, and he couldn't risk it by giving in to his base urges right now.

So, instead of giving the kid exactly what he deserved, he stepped away, placing the bag and its contents exactly as they were when he'd found them.

He knew what he needed to do. At most, this kid was a pawn in all of this. He wasn't even alive when Haley was murdered. This was leading to a bigger fish, and now, Ryan knew just which line to follow to reach him.

"Watch out, Foggy," he said, stepping back to his car before Edwards even came out of the gas station. "I'm coming for you."

Fifteen minutes later saw Ryan back on the road to Foggy's place. He had driven this same lane so many times when he was a kid. Haley had meant so much to him. They had even talked about getting married at one point. Like so many things in life, though, it wasn't meant to be. Ryan was destined for other things, and Haley was destined for a fate that kept him up at night.

Ryan tightened his grip on the steering wheel as he started up the driveway. He might have been trying to keep his continued involvement in this case on the down low. That wouldn't be possible after tonight. Hopefully, it wouldn't matter. He was going to confront Foggy with what he knew, with the proof of his involvement in all of this. He would make him confess. He'd make him admit to the terrible thing he did to his sister.

Rage filled him as he threw the car into park and opened the driver's side door. He was righteous and indignant. Most of all, he was focused and ready.

He stepped out, letting the breeze of the Lowcountry sweep through his hair. It reminded him of her, like she was calling to him. Haley King had called to him so many times. Maybe after tonight, he'd finally be able to answer her.

Then as he took his first step toward the house, a gunshot sounded, filling the air. It seemed Ryan Devereux had come for redemption and found trouble.

Chapter Twenty-Two

Gravel crushed beneath Ryan's feet as he ran up the driveway toward Foggy's house. Being both a detective and a born and raised Southerner, he'd heard his fair share of gunshots. After all these years, it was like instinct. The sound just sent his heart pumping and his feet racing right toward it. He didn't know what was going on or who was in there, but when a gun is fired in someone's house, it's never good.

He turned the handle, pushing through the doorway and into the living room. On the floor lay Foggy, bleeding out and surrounded by a pool of bright red blood. He was struggling to breathe, fighting to stay alive. But one look at him let the detective know that was a fight he was going to lose. Even if emergency medical services were already on their way, they wouldn't be able to make it in time. Not with the amount of blood he'd already lost.

Foggy King would die on his living room floor, almost twenty years to the day after his young sister, whom he may very well have murdered. Looking down at him Ryan, searched his mind for anything he might be able to do to help, but it was pointless. Foggy King was dead.

"Shit!" Ryan said, kneeling down beside him.

Almost as soon as the last breath left his body, a stiff, hot South Carolina breeze blew through the house, sending chills down Ryan's arm. There'd been a time during his youth when his momma would tell him of the Lowcountry winds and how they had the power to take your soul if God wanted it.

'The winds of change . . .' she'd say. *'They're more real than people think. You just watch out for 'em, make sure you're right with Jesus, and they'll pass you by. If not, that change might be so big you won't live to see past it.'*

Maybe his mother was right, and maybe he was too. But that still left him with one nagging question. If Foggy King really were responsible for his sister's murder, then why had it taken so long for the Lord to make it right, and why now? Why this night?

Maybe he'd never been the best person in the world, and maybe he and Ryan had never gotten along too well, but that didn't mean the detective was happy to see him this way. He was, after all, still a citizen, one Ryan had sworn to serve and protect.

"If it was you, I'm going to find out," Ryan said, his eyes focused on the lifeless body at his feet. "But I hope I'm wrong." And now, for all the detective knew, he was. After all, someone shot Foggy. Maybe that someone knew something about Haley.

Perhaps they were even somehow involved in what had happened to her all those years ago.

Reaching into his back pocket and taking out his phone, he began dialing 911 but stopped short of actually pressing the *Send* button. Foggy King was dead, and nothing was going to change that.

"Kit," he said as she answered the phone. "I need you to come out to the King house. To Johns Island—" He stopped, hearing footsteps above him.

"Ryan?" Kit said as he ended the call and slid the phone back into his pocket.

Removing his gun from its holster, Ryan headed up the winding staircase toward Haley's room. The house was dead silent, save for a few small dings as someone moved through what in the beginning he thought was Haley's room. As he reached the top landing of the stairs, however, he realized the sound was coming from a little further down the hall.

Keeping his movement slow and steady, he stepped lightly down the hall toward a large set of French doors. Through the open windows, Ryan heard the sound of a boat clanging against the dock as the waves crashed toward shore. He knew the boat even without looking at it. The King family had bought their boat, *The Irish Lady*, only a few months after Ryan and Haley began dating.

In all the years they'd owned the boat, Ryan knew of its leaving the dock only a handful of times. It seemed very few members of the King family actually enjoyed sailing, most choosing to enjoy their days simply lying on the beach, sipping ice-cold beer, and living the quintessential beach-bum lifestyle, which in Lowcountry was seen as something to aspire to. At least, in Ryan's eyes.

Passing the door to Haley's old room, Ryan paused for a moment, the familiar scent of sandalwood drifting through the air. He kept his ear pressed against the door, but after hearing nothing, he kept moving. The light rattle of something being moved rang out, carrying gently across the hot breeze. Whoever was in the room was doing their best to keep quiet, which likely meant they knew he was coming.

Wrapping his hand slowly around the doorknob and turning the handle, he threw the door open, entering the room with his gun held high, ready to fire. But what he saw wasn't an armed man.

Sitting on the bed with a sock stuffed in her mouth was a young lady. Wearing a pair of faded jeans and a Rolling Stones T-shirt, she looked frightened half to death. Makeup, thick and dark, ran in heavy streaks down her face, mixing with tears. With a look of terror painted across her face, she backed up, trying her best to get as far away from the detective as possible.

"Is there anyone else here?" he asked, keeping his voice low.

The frightened young woman shook her head, then nodded to the open bay window at her side. With a sock wedged in her mouth and fear practically oozing out of her pores, understanding the young woman was nearly impossible. Ryan slowly stepped closer, keeping a finger pressed against his lips, then removed the sock from her mouth.

"My name is Ryan Devereux," he said. "I'm a detective with the Charleston County Police Department. Can you tell me what happened here?"

"A man . . ." she said through tear-filled eyes. "He shot Foggy."

"Did you recognize the man?" Ryan asked.

"No," the woman said. "I'd never seen him, but Foggy knew him. He let him in."

"Was he expecting him?"

"No," she answered. "I . . . I don't think so. We were on a date, and . . . they argued about something. I don't know what. I was in the bathroom."

"Did you see him shoot Foggy?" Ryan asked, placing his hand on her shivering shoulder and trying his best to comfort the young woman.

"Yes," she replied. "From the balcony. The guy . . . he didn't see me. I don't think he knew I was here."

"Then who put the sock in your mouth?" Ryan asked.

"I did. I was on the balcony when he shot him. I hid in the closet so he wouldn't see me. I put the sock in my mouth so I wouldn't scream. When I saw you coming, I was too afraid to remove it," she said, bursting into another round of tears.

"It's okay," Ryan said, pressing her head into his chest. "My partner is on the way. You're okay."

"He went out there." She pointed to the balcony as the sound of a boat engine fired up.

"Wait here," Ryan said, heading for the balcony.

Chapter Twenty-Three

Looking across the dock, Ryan saw the King family's boat bobbing in the waves. The water rippled as dark clouds began to fill the night sky, blocking out most of the moonlight and drenching the shoreline in a new and ominous darkness.

Just a little further down the shore, he spotted another smaller boat beginning to move. A hooded figure stood behind the wheel, though with the moonlight quickly fading, he was only able to see the silhouette of what looked like a tall, thin man.

"I'll be right back." He turned to the young woman, then quickly made his way out of the house and down to the dock.

This wasn't the first time Ryan Devereux had found himself chasing someone through the sweltering Carolina night. He'd been working for the Charleston County Police Department for the better part of fifteen years. Water was a big part of life in the Lowcountry. Because of that, and because of the fact that Ryan lived on one, he knew his way around a boat.

It had been quite a while since Ryan had last set foot aboard *The Irish Lady*, but he remembered the layout well. Haley had enjoyed spending time on that boat. She'd never had the key, though. Haley's father usually kept that locked in his car. Still, the woman knew a thing or two about hotwiring the vessel, and it was intel he'd picked up from her.

As with everything, time had done much to fade those memories. Just like Haley's face, he couldn't remember the exact specifics of what it took to make *The Irish Lady* run without a key. He could only hope that when he boarded the vessel, it would all come back to him.

Stepping off the dock, he quickly ran to the wheel, feeling around for the latch adjacent to the throttle. Two minutes and a few failed attempts later, he managed to get the thing fired up. Massive bubbles emerged from the stern as the engine roared to life. Then, much faster than he should have, Ryan sped away from the dock, leaving wakes that were much too large crashing against the dock.

Moving the throttle forward in a smooth and rapid fashion, the bow leapt from the water, rising higher than the twelve to fifteen degrees he normally shot for. A few seconds later, the boat finally managed to find its plane, making his ride much smoother and allowing him to pick up speed.

A bit further down the coast, Ryan saw the other boat speeding away from him, bobbing up and down as though it was being driven by someone not used to sailing. For Ryan, that was a good thing. At least with the trim incorrect the way it was, they wouldn't be able to pick up too much speed.

As Ryan gained on the boat ahead of him, he began to make out a name written across its hull. "Cecelia . . ." he said to himself, feeling as though he recognized the name.

He hated sailing at night. He always had. Even when he and Haley used to steal the boat, they'd never go more than a few minutes away from the dock. There were just too many things that could go wrong under the cloak of darkness, too much mystery and danger lurking in the marshy water of Lowcountry.

With a hood covering his head, Ryan still couldn't tell who was behind the wheel of the other boat. But the closer he got, the more erratic the driver's behavior became, quickly turning from side to side and creating massive wakes that sent *The Irish Lady* sailing into the air with every turn. Whoever was driving that boat had murdered a man in cold blood, and in his own home.

There was a terror in the waters that night, and not just because Ryan was chasing a criminal but because of what that chase represented. If he managed to get away now, if Ryan managed to lose track of him, then not only would he have to deal with the grief of Haley, but he'd also feel responsible for Foggy. Even though twenty years separated their deaths, the brother and sister would be reunited in the stories Charleston's people would undoubtedly tell after this night. It seemed like something out of a movie, a killer sitting in wait for two decades, just biding his time until his past caught up with him.

But this was no movie. This was all too real. Ryan Devereux was no longer chasing down theories, feelings, and memories. He was chasing down the truth, the truth of who'd killed the girl who'd once meant so much to him, the truth of who'd changed the landscape of Charleston forever. He was chasing down the man who took it upon himself to play God.

"Come on, asshole," Ryan said, slamming his boat into the side of *Cecelia*.

A loud crackling echoed out as the two fiberglass hulls collided, forcing huge wakes out of the water and into the air. Droplets fell from the humid Carolina night like bullets, assaulting him over and over again, covering his face in a sticky wetness as the water mixed with his salty sweat.

"Stop the vessel!" Ryan yelled, seeing the man look over at him from beneath his large black hood. "Stop the vessel! Cecelia!" He yelled out the boat's name.

It was no use, though. His words only seemed to agitate the man even further, causing him to speed up even more until finally, he began to pull away from the detective. "Oh, no, you don't ," Ryan said, pushing hard against the throttle, though it seemed his boat was somehow slowing.

"What the—" He looked down, seeing the fuel gauge pointed to *Empty*. "Oh, no . . ."

Hearing the engine die, Ryan ran to the edge of the bow, watching the man disappear into the dark Carolina night. Only . . . he didn't disappear. The boat came to a stop just a few meters in front of him, then turned back to face his boat. With only the light echo of *Cecelia's* engine in the distant breeze, Ryan watched as the hooded figure stared at him from behind the wheel.

What was he thinking? Was he trying to identify Ryan? Maybe he was planning to make a visit to the detective's house later. Maybe he thought he'd be able to get some revenge, or maybe he was just curious in that strange way twisted people are. Either way, Ryan didn't like the way this was headed.

"Charleston Police Department!" he yelled out. "Please dock your vessel and surrender peacefully!"

The next three minutes were eerily still. It seemed as though just like Ryan, the water was waiting to see what happened next, holding its breath and watching from below its dark, murky surface. Life on the water had always been something of a coin toss, with its unpredictable weather and the strange people it often seemed to attract. But a boat standoff with a murderer topped the list of crazier things he'd seen.

"Wait . . ." he said, seeing a large swell of water emerge from behind *Cecelia*. "Is he . . ." The hooded driver leaned forward, pushing the throttle all the way forward. The boat's bow jetted skyward as it began barreling toward the detective.

He was stuck, out of fuel and unable to move. A sense of fear began to wash over him. In only a second, the boat he stood on would likely be nothing more than a pile of floating rubble and debris. If Ryan didn't act fast, he might not make it out alive.

"Screw this," he said, grabbing a lifejacket and leaping over the boat's starboard side.

Seconds later, a thunderous crash filled the moonless night sky. Fiberglass, metal, and wood all rained down, splashing into the dark water in rapid succession. Taking a deep breath, Ryan turned his head downward, trying to make it below the surface while he still could, though his efforts were too little, too late. A metal rod, large and bent at one end, slammed into the back of his head, submerging him beneath the water's surface as his world went dark.

Chapter Twenty-Four

Haley's beautiful face hovered before him like a dove gliding across the sky. It was dark. There was no moon, yet he could still make out her features. Her hair, lovely and dark, hung across her face like newly-woven silk, and her eyes, bright and wide, stared down at him as he struggled to breathe. He could feel her breath on his skin, hear her words in his ears. She was there with him once again.

"Haley . . ." he tried to say, though speaking came hard.

Water, warm and black, covered his body. Thick Carolina sand clung to his wet skin, holding on for dear life as he lay on the beach. Each wave, each new break in the tide washed against his feet like a familiar visitor, showing up unannounced and unwanted. She placed her hands on his chest, pushing down hard, each time breathing heavily. Her voice, light and soft, carried through the dark air between them, coming to rest on his body like a bird to its nest. He'd missed her for so long, and now she was back.

"Haley . . ." he tried again to mutter. His words were stuck, held hostage by fear and confusion. Where was he? Had she returned or had he left this life behind? And if so, would he be happy in the new land he'd call home?

"Ryan," she said, slapping her hands against his cheek. "Wake up!"

But he was awake. He could feel her, see her, and smell her. Haley knelt next to him, love and kindness pouring from her body like water from the mouth of a river. There'd been so much time, so much heartache and longing since he'd last felt the nearness of her youth. But he'd found it once again, and this time, he wouldn't let go.

"Well . . ." a voice said. "Someone's finally awake."

Ryan's eyes fluttered open as he awakened from his heavy slumber. He felt the cold air dance across his bare chest and arms as he gripped the bed, lumpy and uncomfortable as if it were made of twigs and rocks. He was confused but awake, perhaps more fully awake than he'd ever been. A slow realization fell across him. It was a dream. Haley hadn't been there. She was gone.

"Where am I?" he asked, looking around the room. There was a familiar dread about the place. Its white walls and septic smell seemed all too real as he struggled to sit up. His head felt different somehow, heavier and less familiar than it once had. Looking down, he saw small adhesive badges stuck to his chest, each one with a small, thin wire snaking from it and into a small machine. He was in the hospital. He'd been injured.

"You're in the hospital." Jillian came into view. "Kit pulled you from the water."

"Jillian," he said, a pang of pain shooting down the back of his neck as he turned to meet her eyes. "You're here."

"I drove back as soon as I got the call."

"What call?"

"The one from your partner," she answered, sitting on the edge of his small bed. "Kit called me at about four o'clock in the morning. She said you'd been in an accident. Apparently, she's your emergency contact now."

"The boat . . ." A wave of fresh guilt and broken memories crept into his mind, each one a different piece of the night before, each one stitching itself to the next until finally, he remembered. "Foggy!" he snapped, doing his best to sit up. "He's dead."

"Yes," Jillian replied, pushing him back down. "Take it easy. You're not supposed to—"

"I'm fine."

"You don't look fine." She folded her arms across her chest. "You look like death warmed over."

"I need to get back there."

"Back where?" she asked. "To the house that's now a crime scene? To the boat you destroyed? Or to the beach you nearly died on? Where would you like to go?"

"I saw him," Ryan said. "I saw the murderer."

"You're impossible," she muttered. "Be that as it may, you nearly died. You have to stay here until the doctor releases you. End of story."

"I just want—"

"Shut up!" Jillian exclaimed. "Just shut the hell up, Ryan."

"Jillian, I—"

"No." She pounded her fist into the bed. "Enough is enough! You have to stop this! It's not worth the cost. You're losing too much here . . . and we're losing you!"

"Not worth the cost?" he repeated, stunned that she'd ever say such a thing.

Jillian may have not liked the idea of her husband devoting one hundred percent of his time to work, but she'd never been the type to say someone's life didn't matter. She was a good person, a decent woman with strong Southern morals and a fear of the Almighty. She'd always had his best interest at heart, even when they disagreed about what those interests should be. That was happening today, though Ryan couldn't afford the distraction right now.

"She's dead, Ryan," Jillian said. "I know you loved her, and I know you have this thing where you imagine what your life would have been like if you'd gotten to be with her, but finding her killer isn't going to give you that. It's not going to bring her back."

"It's not for me," Ryan said, surprised at everything his now ex-wife said.

"Then who is it for, Ryan?" she asked. "Because the only family that poor girl had left is in the morgue now too. Who could you possibly be fighting this fight for if not yourself?" She leaned forward and took his hand. "Maybe you really don't see it. Maybe you actually do think this is like every other case to you." She shook her head. "It's not, sweetie. You're not acting like yourself, and that's to be understood. This woman has been your entire life."

Ryan pulled his hand away from Jillian's. Her words slid into him like a sharp knife. "That's not true," he said. "Don't you lay that on me. Don't you insinuate that I was a bad husband or that I'm a bad father. I love our daughter. I loved you, Jilly."

She blinked at him, taking a deep, steadying breath. "That's not what I meant. I know you love her, Ryan, and you are a good father. Haley was your first love, though, and her death is what spurred you to become the man you are now. She might not have been your entire life, but she sure as hell shaped it."

Ryan sighed heavily. "I just want to do my job, Jilly."

"Except this isn't your job anymore, is it?" she asked. "You were taken off this case, right? Kit told me that too."

"There was a misunderstanding," Ryan answered. "It's nothing."

"Nothing?" she asked. "Is nothing why you insisted I take our daughter out of town?"

A lightbulb went off over the detective's head. "Carly," he gasped. "Where is she? Who is she with?"

"I left her with Thomas," Jillian admitted, shaking her head.

"Tell me you're joking," Ryan answered immediately. "Tell me you did not leave our daughter alone with that man."

"That man lives with our daughter day in and day out," Jillian answered. "He's family to her, and whether you like it or not, she's as safe with him as she is with either one of us."

"He's not family," Ryan answered quickly. "He's never going to be her family." He scoffed. "He lied to you! He lied to both of us."

"About an affair with Haley he had a hundred years ago?" Jillian asked. "We were all children then. Besides, I didn't know either of you back then, and I certainly can't hold something a man did before he could even legally drink against him today. He's been good to me, Ryan. He's been attentive and caring, and most importantly, he's been there."

"Unlike me, you mean?" he asked, his jaw tightening.

"It is what it is, sweetie," she answered. "Doesn't mean I want to see you get yourself killed." She stood and headed toward the door. "And just so you know, just because he isn't family now doesn't mean he won't be soon enough."

"I know, the wedding," Ryan said remorsefully. "I guess the mailman misplaced my invitation."

"You can't behave yourself at dinner. What on earth would you do at the wedding?" she asked. "And that's not what I'm talking about. I wasn't sure how to tell you this, and honestly, this doesn't seem like the best time. But I don't want you finding out any other way."

"What is it?" Ryan asked, sitting up in his hospital bed.

"It's me," Jillian answered. "I'm pregnant."

Chapter Twenty-Five

Ryan couldn't think straight for what seemed like a lifetime after Jillian left the room. His head was spinning, his heart was racing, and his entire body seemed to hurt. It was like he had been kicked squarely in the soul. If what his ex-wife just said was true, and Ryan had no reason to believe it wasn't, then the axe that had always been hanging over the shambles of his marriage had finally fallen.

To be honest, he'd never really imagined Jillian would come back to him. In truth, he didn't really want her to. She had betrayed him. She had proven herself unworthy of the love and loyalty he had given her in their decade and a half of marriage. Still, they'd had happy times once. They'd been in love, deeply so, and it hurt to let go of that. What hurt more, of course, was leaving his daughter behind. Though there was no power on this planet that could ever pull him away from Carly completely, Ryan had to admit that when Jillian ended their marriage, it had changed things completely for him. He couldn't live with his daughter in the home he'd built for her anymore.

That house was occupied by another man now, by that bastard who was eating food Ryan paid for and sleeping next to a woman he'd sworn to love for the rest of his life. He would never again wake to the smell of her homemade buttermilk pancakes. He would never again sit next to her and watch the morning sunrise. Someone else would take his place.

And now that man was going to bring one of that woman's children into the world. Whatever false hope Ryan had held of a reconciliation was gone now, completely destroyed.

He was lost in that emotion when the door opened. So lost, in fact, that he didn't even realize his boss was entering the room.

That blessed reprieve ended when the man barked in his direction.

"You've really screwed things up this time!"

Ryan's head jerked up, and his eyes focused on what was going on in front of him. His direct superior officer, Chief Evans, stood in front of him. Where Jillian's eyes had been painted with concern and worry, Chief Evans's held no such weight. His anger was plain on his face and his frustration was at a boiling point.

Their troubled relationship was far from a secret. Practically everyone in Charleston County knew of their feelings about one another. Everyone remembered Ryan for the troubled young man he'd once been. But this was the South, and even though those days were long behind him, the Lowcountry people never seemed to forget.

"Chief," Ryan said, swallowing hard and trying to pull himself together. He could see the man was upset, and it wouldn't take a rocket scientist to figure out why. Still, he had always heard ignorance was bliss. So why not give it a try?

"Is everything all right?"

"Don't play coy with me, you son of a bitch," he shot back. "Do you have any idea how much trouble you're in?"

Okay. So the ignorance thing wasn't exactly bliss this time. But maybe it would be enough to save his hide.

Ryan took a deep breath. "I know what you're going to say." He shook his head.

"You have absolutely no idea what I'm going to say," he answered, nostrils flared. "Because if you did, you'd be running away right now."

The man's emotions practically spewed from his mouth and eyes. Both his words and his stare cut through Ryan like a spear. Chief Evans had never been one to hold back, but today he seemed a little readier to let his emotions loose and to place the blame where he thought it belonged.

"I did what I thought was best, Chief," he said, standing his ground, or more aptly, sitting it. "I was trying to solve this case."

"A case I expressly took you off of," he said. "Do you think I'm stupid, Ryan? Do you think I got my position by accident?"

Ryan always hated those types of arguments, the whole *I deserve my place in this world* crap. Most everyone deserved to be where they were. If they didn't, they wouldn't be there, plain and simple. Sure, there may have been the rare exception, but for the most part, life gives a man what he's earned.

"Of course not, sir," he said, treading lightly as he continued. "It's just—"

"Then why the hell would you think that the orders I give you are optional?" he asked.

It was a stupid question, fueled solely by anger and frustration, though the detective wasn't sure it was directed only at him. He'd known his superior long enough to tell when there was something else under the surface, something even stronger than the juvenile feeling of being pissed off. Chief Evans knew Ryan would soon solve the case. Maybe that's what made him so upset. The thought of having to remove the detective before closing the investigation probably rubbed him the wrong way.

"They're not," he said. "I know they're not. I wasn't trying to disobey you, sir. I was simply—"

"Making trouble for me." He stomped his foot furiously. "Do you have any idea how much property damage you caused with your little high-speed chase? The damn Coast Guard had to come out."

"That wasn't my intention," Ryan answered.

"Of course it wasn't," Chief Evans spat back. "No one's intention is ever to screw things up and fail completely, and that's not even taking into consideration the damn explosion."

"The explosion," Ryan muttered, the memory of it all coming back to him like the waves he was once trapped in. He felt the sharp edge of a piece of cast-off metal pierce his scalp and heard the loud thunderous boom that followed and then felt the uncomfortable sensation of water filling his lungs.

"You've gone too far," Chief Evans said, practically growling at the man. "Everything you've done, everything you've refused to do. It's too much. I can't save you this time."

"Save me?" Ryan asked, a pang of anger mixing in with the pain. "I've gotten further in this investigation than anybody else. The fact that you took me off it is just a testament to how far off the mark you are."

"Frankly," Chief Evans started, "you wouldn't have any idea what we have or have not learned about the case since you were removed. That's privileged information and you've lost your privilege. What's more, you've lost all your privileges as well as your badge."

Ryan stiffened in the bed. "What are you saying?"

"I'm saying you crossed a line, Son," he answered. "My superiors are looking at me for this. I can't allow this to go unpunished. My hands are tied, Ryan. I'm sorry, but I have to suspend you from the police force." He sighed. "Effective immediately."

Chapter Twenty-Six

"Hey there, sweetie." Michelle entered the room.

In the couple of days he'd been in the hospital, Ryan had only managed to see her once, and even then, it was just for a second. But that was mostly because he'd had so much trouble staying awake. But with lying still in a hospital bed, eating crappy food, and getting himself pumped full of more drugs than he actually needed, he wasn't always in the best mood.

"You on break?" he asked, watching her close the door.

She smiled. "Actually, my shift is over. I just thought I'd come check in on you. From what I hear, you'll be out of here in the morning."

"Here's hoping," Ryan responded. "You got your hair cut."

"You like it?" She smiled.

Her once-long hair was cut into a short, spiky, pixie-type thing. While the look may not have worked on a lot of people, it actually looked rather nice on her. With her small frame and light features, she looked like a pixie anyway. Stepping closer, she made a few checks of his vitals, though it looked as if she was killing time more than anything else. Ryan was fine. He knew that. His being there was just a mix of precaution and the fact that he didn't really want to head home.

"I do," he answered as she sat beside him, letting her fingernails lightly stroke his arm.

Ryan felt the hairs on the back of his neck spring up as she thoughtfully grazed his skin, letting herself get lost in his eyes. There'd always been a wonderful smell that carried along with the woman, seeming to almost emanate from her skin. Not too sweet, and just a little spicy, it reminded him of the way a beach smelled just after a bonfire. He'd always been crazy about it, often placing his head against her neck just to get a whiff of the delightful fragrance. He wondered how she might react if he did that now.

"How's your head?" she asked, running her hands through his dark hair and leaning in.

"Better . . ." he answered. "Especially now."

Her lips were soft and warm as they pressed against his. It had been longer than he'd realized since he'd last been touched, much too long, really. But with being so caught up in his work, he hadn't taken the time to feel the closeness of another person. Now that she was there and eager to continue where they'd left off after their last date, he didn't intend to waste the moment, even if he was hooked up to a bevy of machines.

"I've missed you." Her lips grazed his cheek as her sweet, hot breath invaded his ear canal.

Ryan felt his pulse begin to race, causing hot blood to pump through his veins like a raging river. Lifting his hand from beneath the sheets, he placed it on the small of her back, letting his finger slide under her powder-blue scrubs.

"I've missed you too," Ryan answered, letting all of it go. The revelation about his ex-wife had hit him like a ton of bricks. Thomas had gotten her pregnant. He was going to be part of this family now, a real part of it, and there was nothing Ryan could do about it.

He could do something about this though. He could do something about the beautiful and amazing woman who wanted to be closer to him, who appreciated him on so many levels.

"We need to go out again," he said as she wrapped her arms around his neck.

"I thought that was what we were doing now," she purred.

"Detective Devereux," a familiar voice called out from the doorway. "I'm sorry, I didn't mean to . . ."

"That's okay," Michelle said, quickly pulling away. "I was just leaving." She turned back to Ryan. "You know where to find me."

"What are you doing here?" Ryan asked, seeing Mr. Abernathy walk through the door.

"I just wanted to stop by and check on you, to make sure you were okay," he said, placing a white plastic bag on the counter. "I picked you up some chicken and waffles from that little place on the corner."

"Jestine's?" Ryan asked. "Thank you, but you didn't have to do that."

"It's not a problem," his former professor answered. "I heard what happened to you. Something about a boat explosion?" He cocked his head to the right.

"Yes," Ryan answered. "I was working a case when . . . it's a long story."

Truth be told, Ryan had relived that moment enough. The last thing he wanted to do was go through it all again. Though he had a feeling that wouldn't matter too much to Rufus. He'd always been one to live for the details, to ask every little mundane question he could think of, no matter the subject matter.

"I've got time," he answered.

"Well," Ryan sighed. "I was visiting Foggy King when I heard a gunshot. I ran inside but by the time I got there, he'd already been shot. He died almost instantly."

"That's terrible," Rufus said. "Do you have any idea why someone would want to murder Foggy?"

"No," Ryan answered, thoughts of the young man he'd followed entering his mind. "It's odd that it happened so close to the anniversary of his sister's death, but at the moment, I haven't got much to go on." He lied, deciding to keep the information about the young kid quiet. "It's just difficult to reopen that box, the one you've spent so long making sure was airtight in the back of your mind, the one that hides all of your secrets so they can't hurt you. Unpacking it and bringing it into the light is something I really wasn't prepared to do."

"I know what you mean." Rufus looked to the floor, his eyes beginning to fill with tears. "I can't help but think about my daughter now, about what she'd look like today. I wonder if she'd like country music, if she'd prefer seafood above steak . . . simple things."

"Yes," Ryan said. "It can be hard."

The truth was, Ryan had completely forgotten about his former professor's wife and daughter. He'd only mentioned them once or twice in the entire time they'd known one another, and even then, it was only for a second or two. He understood, though. Memories like those become more painful with each spoken word.

"They never caught the guy?" Ryan asked. "Right?"

"Never," Mr. Abernathy answered. "The case remains unsolved."

"Just like Haley." Ryan looked to him.

"Yeah," he said. "I guess so."

Sadness is a terrible thing, but grief is the worst of things, at least to Ryan. Plain sadness can be alleviated with something as simple as a visit from a friend. Grief, on the other hand, has no relief. There's no magic pill, no classic movie, nothing but time and painful introspection that can relive the trauma of losing someone.

"I miss her every day," Rufus said. "I miss them both. If I'd have just been there. If I'd have gotten home earlier, then maybe they would have gone for that walk. Maybe they'd still be alive today."

Ryan was much too young to remember what had happened to his family, much too preoccupied with toys and board games to ever care about the news or the stories it contained. He was happy in his childish ignorance, and knowing what he knew now, he wished he could have found a way to stay in that bubble.

"There were no witnesses." Rufus sighed. "No one saw anything. How can that be?"

"That doesn't mean the case would have been solved," Ryan replied. "Just look at what happened to me with Foggy. I have a witness. She saw the murderer and I still don't know anything."

"Witness?" Rufus tilted his head.

"Yeah," Ryan replied. "There was a woman there. She was on a date with Foggy. She said—"

"Ryan?" Kit's voice called out from the doorway. "Are you awake?

"Yeah" he replied. "Come on in."

Mr. Abernathy stood from his chair, staring at his former student for a long minute. "I'll go," he said finally. "I just wanted to bring the chicken. We'll have dinner once you're out."

"Sounds good."

Kit Walker entered the room, slowly at first. It was almost as if she was expecting some sort of response from her partner, as if he'd been waiting for her return so he could give her a piece of his mind or something. But after a moment, she seemed to ease up a bit, shaking off the tension in her bones.

"I've come to take you home."

Chapter Twenty-Seven

"You sure you don't need me to come in?" Kit asked.

"No," Ryan assured her. "I'm good. A few Advil and a good night's sleep in my own bed and I'll be fine. Thanks for the offer, though, and thanks for driving me home."

"No problem," she answered, watching him open the door.

Kit wanted to say so much, to tell him that if she were being honest with him, and more importantly, herself, she thought he shouldn't have been suspended. That wasn't her battle, though, not her mountain to climb or her war to wage. But that didn't mean she was without opinion. Ryan had come to mean a lot to her. It was he who'd first introduced her to sweet tea. Real sweet tea, that is, the kind you can only get in the South. Not like that canned crap they had up north where she was from.

It was Ryan who'd slowly taught her how to relax on the beach and not feel guilty about it. He taught her how to shuck an oyster and how to slow down and appreciate time before it managed to pass her by. He'd taught her what it was like to live in and be part of the South, and for that, she would be forever thankful.

"Are you sure?" she repeated, then stopped short. "I could just—"

There, on the docks, stood Michelle Myers, the object of Ryan's on-again, off-again romance. Her short yellow hair glistened in the evening sky, catching what looked like every ray of sunlight and reflecting it back across the water. With the ocean at her back and Ryan Devereux walking toward her, Kit couldn't help but be a little bit jealous.

It wasn't everyday she felt envious of another woman. She usually thought of that kind of thing as beneath her. But after knowing Ryan, after seeing the softer, quieter side of him, she began to feel something swell inside her. It wasn't love, that much she knew. Love was for children. It was something else. There was a safety in Ryan, a comfort she hadn't felt in some time, and as she watched him wrap his arms around Michelle, she slowly began to realize maybe she was ready to find that comfort again.

"Goodnight, Kit," he called.

"Goodnight, Ryan," she answered, watching him disappear in her rearview mirror.

Not quite ready to head home, Kit decided to make a stop at a small bar along the way to her house. Sure, the Lowcountry bar scene was a bit different from the one back home in New Jersey, but at least the drinks were cheap. There, she'd never managed to know the bartender's name, even though the same overweight bald guy had been pouring her drinks since moving to the small neighborhood she'd called home.

In the South, though, it was a whole different story. Since the first moment she'd stepped foot in Charley's Hideaway, she'd had an open tab and a room full of people willing to get to know her. It took a while to get used to, and in the beginning, talking so openly to people she'd just met made her a little uncomfortable. But after living in Charleston County for a few months, she began to appreciate the chatty locals and their easygoing nature.

"Kit," Charley said from behind the bar. "Haven't seen you in a few days."

"Yeah," she replied. "I've been a little busy."

"So I hear . . ." Charley answered, sliding an ice-cold Corona her way. "I read about Ryan crashing that boat. They said it could be heard two miles away."

"Oh, yeah?" Kit smiled. "Did you hear it?"

"I live three miles from shore . . ."

"So close." She snapped her fingers.

"Story of my life."

Charley Charles was a kind man with a deep voice and a big bear-like presence about him. She'd always found him warm and inviting, and just like almost everyone else in Lowcountry, he was ready and willing to listen to anything Kit had to say. In Jersey, she'd have never let her guard down enough to even think she was feeling lonely, let alone say it out loud. But here in the damp heat of South Carolina, the words just seemed to want to spill out.

"Kit," Jackson said, plopping himself down at the bar before she had a chance to speak.

"Jackson." She turned to him. "Haven't seen you in a while."

"I feel like that's a running theme around here the last few days," Jackson answered, running a hand through his thick, lustrous hair. "I went almost an entire day without seeing my sister earlier this week. Then, yesterday, I realized I hadn't seen Ryan in two days. It's crazy."

"Yeah," Kit replied, trying her best to sound genuine. "That's . . . a long time."

In New Jersey, not seeing someone you know, family or otherwise, for a week or two was perfectly normal. But here, just a day without a phone call or a stop-by from your friend and people began to panic. It was at once lovely and odd.

"Right?" He raised an eyebrow. "It's good to see you though. How have you been?"

"Good," she replied, managing to hold back the world of emotion trying its best to spill out from her. "I've been good."

"What about Ryan?" he asked. "I meant to get up to the hospital yesterday to see him, but I got caught up helping Patty Parker. Poor thing got her car stuck in the marsh. Took me nearly all day to get the thing free."

"Patty Parker?" Kit asked, feeling a little unfamiliar with the name.

"Yeah," Jackson answered, pointing toward the coast. "She lives out on Old Mill Road. She's got them two kids from that fella from Hilton Head. The one with the new red SUV."

"Right," she said, pretending to know.

Jackson Bennett was, for all intents and purposes, a nice guy, not to mention just about as easy on the eyes as anyone Kit had ever seen. Sitting across from him and watching his full lips ramble on about the people of Charleston, she felt that wave of loneliness rise up inside her once again. But she'd heard about Jackson, about the many girls his good looks and winning smile had afforded him, so with a deep breath, she managed to dispel that wave once again, choosing to stand, thank him for the lovely conversation, and head home.

Chapter Twenty-Eight

It's often said that you can't leave Charleston without visiting Battery Park, and having grown up just a mile from its picturesque breezy shores, Ryan Devereux understood that statement completely. A fantastic stretch along the city's southern tip, the row of antebellum-style mansions overlooking Charleston Harbor was once the heart and soul of the city's maritime activity. But as time went on and the world began to change around it, Battery Park drew more tourists than shrimp boats.

Bordered by the Ashley and Cooper Rivers, it was one of the detective's favorite places in all the city. As a child, he'd loved hearing his uncle tell him vibrant tales of the historic battles that once took place along its harbors. For the people of Lowcountry, it was known as White Point Gardens due to the bleached white oyster shells that gathered along its shores every morning. They'd always reminded him of his mother due to her affinity for jewelry making. Each time he'd come home with a baseball cap full of shells, she'd wrap her arms around him and kiss his head. Those days were among his favorite childhood memories. He was so happy then, so innocent and green to the harsh ways of humanity.

Slowly sipping a glass of whiskey and listening to the call of the ocean, Ryan wondered just how he'd gone from that innocent little boy to the jaded man he was now. The world was a tough place, sure . . . but did that really mean he had to let it change him so fundamentally? Did he have to give in to its whims the way he had?

He wasn't sure. Though with his mind as chaotic as it was, he really wasn't sure of much else either. All Ryan knew was that unless he got to the bottom of this thing, unless he figured out who was responsible for the murders of two innocent people, he'd never have another restful night's sleep. He owed it to Foggy and Haley. He owed it to his Lowcountry home.

"You haven't said a word," Michelle said, gently nudging his hand with hers.

"Oh," Ryan replied. "I'm sorry. I've just been thinking about Battery Park."

"Battery Park?" Michelle asked. "Why?"

In truth, Ryan wasn't sure what had spurred the thoughts of his childhood. Perhaps it was his mind's way of trying to keep the investigation away from him. He couldn't help it, though. He couldn't help thinking about her and about the case. Pictures of her face, memories from that past . . . they were like sharks in the water, circling his mind with the crest of every new wave, just waiting for the boat to tip, letting them devour him. He had to do something.

"I'm going to the station," he said to Michelle.

"What?" she asked. "Do you really think that's wise?"

"I have to," he answered. "I've been thinking about it. Something just doesn't make sense. Haley was seeing Thomas Kent around the same time she was seeing me. But he was out of town that week. He missed prom."

"What are you saying?" Michelle asked.

"I'm saying she must have been seeing more than just me and Thomas."

"Wow," Michelle said. "She got around."

"It was complicated." Ryan sighed. "We were on and off with every turn of the tide. As soon as news got out that we broke up, guys would swoop in, giving her a shoulder to cry on. She was young and didn't know any better."

"So you think she was seeing multiple guys?"

"That's the thing. We were broken up for almost a month before prom. I was dating Katy Harren. It stands to reason that she'd have been seeing someone too," Ryan said. "I just don't know who."

"What good is going to the station gonna do?" Michelle asked.

"I'm not sure, but Chief Evans said something the other day that stuck with me. He mentioned my not knowing what the investigation has turned up. I need to see those files."

"Do you need me to come with you?" she asked, a sweet mix of concern and hesitation in her voice.

Not that the detective wanted or needed company while sneaking into his workplace, but even if he had, Michelle wouldn't have been his first choice to come along. She had medical training, yes, but he doubted she had much in the way of investigative chops.

"No. I need to go this alone," Ryan answered as the two shared a drink before going their separate ways.

Stepping out of his car, Ryan took note of the unusually cool Carolina evening. His mother used to call them 'barefoot days'. They came a couple of times a month, always out of the blue. It was like mother nature's gift to the Lowcountry, just a simple way to remind people to go outside and have a walk around town, to feel the sand and the grass under their feet and just enjoy God's gift of good food, kind people, and ocean views.

The Charleston County Police Department sat perched near the water at the corner of Lockwood Drive and Fishburne Street with wonderful views of both the Ashley River and the city's beautiful and historic downtown area. From his office window, Ryan could even catch a view of the ocean at high tide. He just never imagined he'd be sneaking into that office in the middle of the night, that's all.

The evidence locker was a big place, but thanks to Chief Evans's almost OCD-like way of handling things, Ryan knew finding the evidence wouldn't be difficult. Just a few minutes after getting in the building, he was standing face to face with a small brown box labeled *Case 17378/King*. He opened the box and sorted through its contents until finding the letters, and there it was, the proof he'd been looking for, only it hadn't been in the letters at all.

In the box was a textbook with Haley's name on it. He recognized her handwriting immediately. The young woman always finished her name with a heart where a *'y'* should have been. And on the front of the book was a Post-It note with the word *Margins* written across it. His eyes grew wide when he began flipping through the pages. The proof of Haley's killer would be in the book. He just needed a little time to read it.

Chapter Twenty-Nine

"Find what you're looking for?" Kit asked.

"Kit!" He turned, nearly frightened out of his skin. "How did—"

"I followed you," she said. "I knew you wouldn't be able to let this go, so I hung around outside the docks. And would you look at that? I was right."

Ryan had known most of Charleston's residents his whole life. He knew their mannerisms, their thought processes, and their instincts. But with Kit Walker, it was a different story. She hadn't been raised in the South. She didn't come from the same Lowcountry stock as everyone else around town, and as a result, he still hadn't learned to completely read her, though he did trust her.

"I have to do this," he answered.

"I'm working on it," she said flatly. "I told you I'd keep the case going, and I have."

"The book." He held out the textbook. "Where did this come from?"

"I found it in the house," Kit answered. "While you were out blowing up boats."

"We searched her room," Ryan answered.

"It wasn't in her room. It was just lying on the living room floor."

"Damn. Why didn't you tell me?"

"You're off the case," she answered. "And it didn't pertain to Foggy, whose case I have no information on, by the way. Thank you for that."

"I'm going to solve this," he said.

"No!" she snapped. "You need to stop this. You need to let it go."

"I can't do this . . ."

"The case?"

"No," Ryan said. "This. I can't argue with you again. I can't keep swimming against the current like this, but I can't let it go. I have to solve this thing. I just won't argue about it anymore."

The purse of her lips slowly began to lessen and her features softened a little bit. It seemed the anger pulsing through her veins was finally dissipating, that she finally, after all this time, understood she wouldn't be able to stop him. Or maybe the Lowcountry air had finally done its job in helping her to understand her partner.

"Let me come with you," she said after a few minutes.

"No," Ryan answered. "I'm in enough trouble with the department now. There's no need in pulling you down with me. You need to keep your distance."

"I'm already an accomplice," she answered. "I'm watching you take evidence."

"Not if you leave. Just walk out that door and pretend you never saw anything."

"I can't do that," she replied. "I'm in this now. I—"

"What?" Ryan's eyes widened.

"There's someone coming," she said, pulling her partner closer and pressing her lips against his.

Her soft hands pulled at his shoulders, bringing him quickly into her. He felt her chest press against his, quickly wrapping him in a fragrant warmth. Her lips were soft and moist as they pressed against his, her tongue gliding across his, searching him for whatever it could find.

"Oh, sorry!" A man entered the room. Ryan recognized him immediately as Henry Kade, the overnight janitor. He'd worked there for a few years, though the two had only spoken a handful of times. "I was just checking. Sorry." He shut the door, exiting the room.

"What was that?" Ryan asked.

"It was the only thing I could think of—"

"No," Ryan said. "That was something else. You kissed me like—"

"No," she interrupted. "I assure you, it was just something to distract Henry."

He wasn't sure he believed her. Of course, he could see where she was coming from. Had he seen Henry coming, he likely would have done the same thing. It was more about the kiss itself. There was something there, something more than just a way to get the janitor out of the room. There were feelings in that kiss. He knew it.

"Fine," he said, not fully believing her but also not wanting to waste any more time talking about it. "Let's just leave it alone."

"Probably best," his partner answered, wiping her lips and looking deep into his eyes. "I'll leave if that's what you really want."

"It is." He sighed. "I can't risk you too."

Kit slowly turned, leaving the room and Ryan behind her. In his life, he'd seen more than a few people turn and walk away. But watching it happen now hit him a little harder than he was expecting. But as the door swung closed, he caught sight of Kit looking back at him, the slight smile on her face, the little twinkle in her eye . . . it was just enough to let him know that this time was different. This time, the woman walking away from him was doing it because she cared, because he'd asked her to.

Chapter Thirty

Back on his houseboat, Ryan's mind was racing. He now knew he was right to think there was something else in the evidence locker. Though it broke his heart to know it, the truth was that Haley had been having multiple affairs when they were together as teenagers. Yes, they were on and off more than a light switch, but it was just sort of an unspoken truth between them that they were supposed to end up together. Everyone in Charleston County knew that.

There was Thomas, of course, who would go on to repeat the process with Ryan's own wife, but he wasn't the important person right now. As much as Ryan would have liked to have seen that particular bastard behind bars, the truth was that Thomas hadn't been responsible for Haley's death. That didn't mean the other person she was sleeping with wasn't, though.

In fact, as Ryan went through the secret notes left in the margins of the textbook he'd taken from the evidence locker, the detective in him concluded that the person writing these notes was probably the person with Haley's blood on his hands. That fact became more and more apparent with each turn of the page.

It was all right there, written in aged ink on the edges of the pages. There were many notes. Some of them were love letters, graphic and inappropriate for someone of Haley's young age. Others were more stressful. They spoke of problems, of the dangers of the relationship they had been having.

If my wife finds out, she'll divorce me. She'll take my daughter, and she'll ruin me. My entire career would go down the toilet, Haley. You know I love you, but I can't risk that.

Ryan's mind twisted like sails in the wind as he wrapped it around the truth. Not only was Haley sleeping with someone, but that someone had been older. He had been a married father, with a wife and a daughter and a job he didn't want to lose. The thought disgusted Ryan both as a detective and as a father. He thought of his own young daughter and how upset he'd be if she were found to be dating an older man. He thought about what he'd say and what he'd do. It wouldn't be good.

Ryan's stomach turned. The idea of that, of someone using his influence to seduce Haley, to convince her that this sort of relationship was in her best interest, was a betrayal of the highest order. It took a specific kind of person to abuse their power in such a way, the worst kind of person.

He took a deep breath and continued reading.

He went through pages and pages of that sort of thing. As hard as it was to swallow for Ryan, as the mystery man became more distant, Haley's notes got clingier, more desperate.

I can't live without you. I know that I promised I'd be stronger than this, but I can't. It's too much. I dreamt about you last night. It was the best dream of my entire life. We were on a boat, sailing away from everything and everyone. That could be real. That could be our everyday.

Ryan grimaced. How could he have been so blind? How could he not have known what was going on right under his nose all those years ago? Had he really been such a different person back then? Was he ever so innocent, so naïve to believe that all people were good?

The notes from the mystery man grew harder and harder until finally, they became downright disturbing. His stomach turned and his head began to ache more with each sentence.

Stop contacting me like this, Haley. I know you were outside my house last night. I saw your car. Do you have any idea how risky that is? Do you know what could happen if anyone found out? It would be bad for both of us. What do you think your future would look like if all of this came out? You'd be branded a whore. No one would be seen with you. That would be the end of things. So just let it go before something bad happens. Don't make me say this to you again.

He read on, surprised by the illicit story playing out before him. His mind began to wander back in time, slowly at first until suddenly, he found himself standing in the Lowcountry marsh, watching it all play out.

I can't let you go. I have to have you, and if the secrecy is what's keeping us apart, then I'll get rid of that too. I'll bring everything out into the open. Think about it. It'll be bad for a little while, but then people will accept it. They accept everything. It might be strange at first, but we can be together, and that's what's important.

The last note, one from the mystery man, simply read,

We need to talk.

Ryan closed the book, his head spinning. This man was married, he was in a position of power over Haley, and their correspondence happened chiefly in school textbooks.

Even though he knew it was true, even though he had stone-cold proof in his hands, he still couldn't believe what he was thinking, but he was thinking it all the same. It was insane, but it was a thread that had to be followed.

He picked up his phone and dialed a familiar number.

"Hey," he said as the man answered. "I'm doing much better. Thank you. Can you do me a favor, though? I'd really like to see you. Can you come over here?" He nodded, listening to the man. "Now is good."

Then he hung the phone up and waited. Ryan Devereux had a sneaking suspicion that all of this was going to end tonight, one way or another.

Chapter Thirty-One

A knock came on the door of Ryan's houseboat, sending his heart jumping into overdrive. He was here. This was happening.

The smell of fried chicken wafted through his houseboat. While he'd never been the best cook in the world, he'd learned enough from his mother to know how to cook up a few signature southern dishes. It may have been a little too late for dinner, but Ryan just felt the need to have something on the table. That, and cooking always helped calm his nerves.

Placing a serving plate on the table, Ryan steadied himself and headed toward the door. He passed by the spot on the floor where he'd found his uncle bleeding and steeled himself. If this man was responsible for any of this, then he was responsible for all of it. He might have had a soft spot in his heart for the man, but if he was a monster, then Ryan would treat him as such.

Ryan pulled the door open to find Mr. Abernathy standing there. He had a smile on his face and a bottle of wine in his hands, a bottle just like the one he'd seen in Foggy's house, just like he'd seen in the boy's car that day. His heart broke. The truth was unfolding in front of his eyes, forever changing the way he viewed two people.

"You brought the wine," he said, nodding mournfully but plastering on a fake smile to stave off any suspicion the man might have. The humid southern air seemed to thicken almost instantly, creating a chasm of mistrust and deceit between them.

"You did ask me for it," Rufus said, not waiting for Ryan to invite him in before he pushed through the doorway. "I'm glad you did too. Feeling well enough to drink means you're feeling better indeed."

"Right as rain," Ryan said as he watched him walk toward the kitchen table. "Things are starting to click into place. I noticed the front of your car is dented. I was involved in a hit and run the other day myself."

"Really?" the professor asked. "I hope everything is okay."

"Oh, yes," Ryan answered. "Just fine."

"Glad to hear it," Rufus said, turning to meet his former student. "How is the case going?"

"Haley's case?" Ryan asked, swallowing hard. "I'm not actually on it anymore. It's for the best, I suppose. I think it was starting to get to me."

"Can't have that," Rufus said, looking around the kitchen. "Do you have a corkscrew in this thing? You know, I always thought it was so strange that you live on this boat." He shook his head.

"Really?" Ryan asked, glaring at the man and wondering if this man, a man he had come to respect so much, could actually be responsible for something as evil as murder. "Don't you have a boat? I thought I remembered something about your buying one a few years back."

"I did," Rufus answered, looking around the kitchen to find the corkscrew. "But it's more to fish in than anything else, I suppose."

Ryan walked closer to him. As he did, he caught a whiff of sandalwood.

"That's a distinctive cologne you're wearing, Professor Abernathy," he said, reaching toward his belt to grab at his gun.

"It's new," he said, and Ryan could sense a hint of tension in his voice.

"You know, I think I've bitten off more than I can chew here," he said, his head still turned toward an open drawer and his hand still on the bottle of wine. "I have a corkscrew at home. Why don't I run back there, pick it up, and pop back over?"

"Don't be ridiculous," Ryan said, settling behind the man with his hand on his gun. "Stay awhile."

"I don't think so," Rufus said.

"Professor Abernathy," Ryan started. "You had a daughter, didn't you?"

"I have the retirement dinner tonight, Ryan," Rufus said, still turned toward the cabinetry. "That's why I'm dressed like this. I'm afraid I have to run."

"What is her name?" Ryan asked. "What is your daughter's name?"

"I think you know," Rufus said, his voice a deep growl.

"Cecelia," Ryan answered. "Professor, I'm going to need you to put your hands up. You're disgusting!" Ryan scoffed. "You gave Haley those little porcelain figurines, didn't you? You broke into my house to get them back, and you paid that kid to do your dirty work."

He watched as Rufus's body stiffened. Then, before he could react, Rufus turned quickly, swinging the wine bottle and slapping him across the face with it.

Ryan fell backward, his gun firing into the ceiling. As he stumbled to the floor, Rufus kicked the gun away. Then, leaning over him, he pulled the wine bottle back, ready to strike.

Before he brought it down on Ryan, knocking him out clean, he muttered something Ryan could barely hear.

"Damn cops."

The detective's world went dark, leaving him swimming in an endless void of blackness, interrupted only by the sound of waves slamming against the shore. He'd been right. The worst thing he could have imagined about his former professor had come to fruition right in his kitchen. And now, if he wasn't able to stop it, he might be the man's third victim.

Chapter Thirty-Two

Ryan's eyes fluttered open. "What . . . what happened?"

The night air was dense. A thick fog hovered over the water as Ryan and his former professor sped further and further into the dark ocean waters. He still couldn't believe where he was. He couldn't believe he was actually right, that this man could kill two innocent people just to protect his dirty secret.

"You couldn't leave well enough alone." Rufus gritted his teeth. "You couldn't just let sleeping dogs lie."

"You should be ashamed of yourself," Ryan snapped, trying his best to wriggle his arms free from their ties. "You're sick. You're a murderer."

"A murderer, yes," Rufus answered, pushing harder on the throttle. "But sick . . . no. I'm just fine. I know exactly what I'm doing."

"She was seventeen!" Ryan snapped. "That's criminal!"

"She was wise beyond her years. That girl was—"

"Don't tell me what she was!" Ryan yelled, his voice getting lost to the rushing wind. "You didn't deserve to know her!"

"And you did?" Mr. Abernathy snarled. "You were too confused and scatterbrained to ever do anyone any good at all. Look at you . . . divorced, fired, and now, about to die."

A warm mist blew high in the air, covering his face and arms. He needed to get free of his restraints and get this proof back to Chief Evans. He needed to give Haley's story the end it deserved.

"And look at you," Ryan said, his blood beginning to boil. "A rapist and a murderer. Why is it that you kept in touch with me all these years? Was it just to keep up with the case?"

"Partially," Rufus answered as the boat bobbed up a bit. "I knew if any information came to light, you'd let me know. I just wasn't expecting her body to be found."

"Why Foggy?" Ryan answered. "What did he have to do with anything?"

"He figured it out," Rufus responded. "He found the textbook Haley and I used to communicate. He was going to turn it in to the police. He blackmailed me, took me for all I had. I didn't have anything else to give him, and I couldn't let him turn me in. I had to do something."

"You piece of shit," Ryan said. "You should have owned up to your crime, not hid behind it like some coward."

"You have no idea what it's like, Son. I've been a pillar of this community since before you were pissing your diapers. I built myself up from nothing. I would have lost my house, my wife, my position in the community. They'd have made me a sex offender. My wife would have taken our daughter away from me." He scoffed. "One little girl ain't worth all that, no matter how pretty she is."

"How can you live with yourself?" Ryan's lip curled. "How can you defend those actions?"

"I don't do things I can't defend, Ryan." His lips began to rise in a half-smile. "I hold fast and true to every decision I make. Unlike you."

"Me?"

"Yes, Son. You!" He looked to his one-time student. "You couldn't even keep the promise you made in front of God."

Jillian's face flashed through his mind, causing an electric pang of pain to shoot across his chest. He hadn't given up on her and he never would. For them, being apart was the better option, that's all. But he'd never once considered walking away from his child. She meant too much.

"God?" Ryan said. "How can you even dare to mention God?"

"Sacrifices must sometimes be made. Everyone understands that, Him especially."

"No." Ryan steadied his voice. "Not like Haley, not like Foggy. Not in South Carolina."

"It doesn't matter now," Rufus said, stepping away from the wheel. "It's in the past and there's nothing we can do about it. I, for one, won't worry."

"How nice," Ryan answered. "To be so confident and unaffected by the loss of two innocent lives. I can't do that."

"You won't have the chance," he replied, taking a lifeboat from the storage door. "I like you, Ryan. I do. You were always a smart kid. I've enjoyed our time together, but I can't let you mess this up for me. I won't spend the rest of my life behind bars for something that happened twenty years ago."

"What about Foggy?" Ryan asked. "That was two days ago!"

"Collateral damage," Rufus said. "But like I said, I've got a dinner to get to, one where everyone in Charleston County will be celebrating me for all the things I've brought to this place. I've done so much good, and you want to destroy all that because of just a little bit of evil. Those numbers don't add up."

"You're going to jail," Ryan said.

"And you have three minutes," Rufus answered.

"What happens in three minutes?"

"This boat will collide with the Morris Lighthouse. Then . . . boom! I'd say it's been nice knowing you, but let's be realistic, shall we?" Mr. Abernathy smiled, tied a belt around the boat's wheel to lock it in place, then grabbed a paddle and his lifeboat before leaping into the dark waters just off the coast.

"Shit!" Ryan said, struggling to get to his feet.

His hands and ankles were tied, though he'd been working his ropes against a particularly sharp edge of the boat's gunwale for the last few minutes. With his heart beating out of his chest and black water spraying in his face, Ryan began rubbing the ropes harder and harder against the small piece of metal.

Morris Island Lighthouse hadn't been active in years so there was no way for the detective to know how much time he had left. Not to mention, the land used to build the structure had been swallowed up by the Atlantic waters sometime in the late sixties, so there would be nothing to slow the boat before the crash, resulting in a strike that would likely send the thing falling into the water.

He wasn't sure if it was the boat or divine intervention, but something managed to break his ropes free at what he could only assume were seconds before the crash. Leaping to his feet, Ryan ran toward the navigation controls just as the clouds dissipated and the moonlight shone through. There was no more time. He was only a few hundred feet from the lighthouse.

Unable to free the knot left by his professor, Ryan pulled hard at the belt. He felt his muscles straining and the fibrous tissue surrounding them tearing until finally, the leather snapped. Flying backward, Ryan crashed hard against the boat's stern as it quickly turned starboard, sending him flying out into the water.

Cold liquid filled his lungs and nostrils and salt burned his eyes as he sank under the water. The quick shock of a cold chill ran up his body, cutting into him like a thousand knives before he managed to make it above the surface, gasping for air. In the distance, he saw the white light of the boat vanish into the night sky. He'd managed to avoid the lighthouse, though he'd paid a price in the form of an elbow-to-wrist gash running along his forearm. Not to mention, he'd lost the professor.

Quickly taking stock of his surroundings, Ryan began the painful process of swimming back to shore. Salt burned his wound as the water around him filled red with blood. The swim was slow, and after a few strokes, his left arm became more dead weight than anything else until finally, he felt the sandy shore under his chest.

"Kit . . ." he said, bringing the phone to his ear. "Morris Island. I need a ride."

Chapter Thirty-Three

"Is that really necessary?" Kit asked as she stepped into the living room.

"It's a retirement dinner," Ryan answered. "I want to look good for it. Did you get everything done?"

"Yes," Kit replied. "We could have just arrested him, you know. Were the theatrics really needed?"

"After everything I've gone through to get this proof, I need them to see. It's the only way they'll understand. Besides, he was right about his reputation. Rufus is beloved around these parts. I can't take the chance that the affection these people feel for him will result in an innocent verdict once it comes to that."

"The citizens?" She raised an eyebrow in confusion. "They'll understand if we arrest him."

"No, they won't," Ryan answered. "You still don't get it, Kit. This is the South, Lowcountry, below the Mason-Dixon . . . however you want to say it. But the point is that these people are different. Rufus Abernathy has been a prominent member of this society for years. The people in town, the ones with any power, half of them were once his students. If they don't see it, if people don't see them seeing it, then they won't believe it. It has to be this way. And this is the perfect place to do it."

"Fine," she answered. "Have it your way."

He'd heard about it weeks ago. The retirement dinner for his former professor was big news in the local Charleston scene. Rufus Abernathy was well-known around town, having mentored both a local judge and two police officers aside from Ryan. Everyone knew him, and as a result, the place would be packed. It was the perfect setting to reveal him for the murdering sicko he was.

"Let's go," Ryan said, stepping onto the dock with Kit right behind him. "It should be starting right about now."

The two got into Ryan's car with him behind the wheel and Kit at his side. He looked at her for a minute. He wanted to ask her about that kiss, the one they'd shared back at the station, but he held off, deciding that maybe that conversation would be better suited for another night. Ryan shifted the car into drive and sped away.

The retirement dinner was to be held in the ballroom of The Grand Tide, one of Charleston's nicest beachside resorts. Once, about a year before, Ryan was called to the hotel after a bar fight got too out of hand. He hadn't paid much attention to the place aside from thinking the massive crystal chandelier hanging in the lobby seemed a bit over-the-top for the area. This, after all, was the heart of Lowcountry, not Miami Beach.

Speeding down highway 171, the two were headed right for Folly Beach where Ryan had big plans for Mr. Abernathy, ones he was sure would make a splash with the people of Charleston County in a way they hadn't seen coming.

As his car crossed the Folly River Bridge, the detective took note of the water, of how much calmer and brighter it seemed now that he was suspended above it as opposed to sinking beneath it. He looked at Kit, again almost mentioning the kiss but again holding back.

"What?" Kit asked, a half-smile stretching across her face.

"What?"

"You look like you want to say something. Or that you're trying not to."

"No," he lied. "I was just looking. I meant to thank you for coming to get me and for tending to my arm."

"We're going to the hospital after this," she answered. "That thing needs stitches."

"Fine," he replied. "After this asshole is behind bars, I'll get stitches."

Bringing his car to a stop a few feet away from the hotel doors, Ryan stepped out, followed closely by his partner. He wore a fitted navy suit and tie with shining black shoes. His hair was brushed back in a perfect wave, with a light spike peeking up from a cowlick he'd had since childhood. Kit stood next to him, her hair hanging straight and slick around her wonderfully proportioned face.

Stepping into the ballroom, Ryan felt two hundred pairs of eyes turn to him. He was late, yes, but it was something more than that. This was the direct result of everything he'd spent the last two weeks doing. The fight with Thomas, the explosion in the water, and the talk around town of the girl found dead. The same girl who'd stood him up for prom all those years ago. There were still people who believed Ryan was responsible, yes. But that was about to change.

"Ryan." Rufus Abernathy's eyes widened to the size of quarters. "Welcome." A nervous fake smile painted itself across his face.

"What's the matter, Mr. Abernathy?" The detective smiled wide. "You look like you've seen a ghost."

Ryan walked toward him, knowing Kit had snuck off into the back room to lay the trap that was about to snare the revered professor.

"Do you know who you're playing with?" Rufus asked.

"Of course, I do," Ryan answered, shaking the man's hand and squeezing it tightly. "You're the man who tied me to a speeding boat and left me to die. You're the man who murdered a man in the foyer of his home while his girlfriend watched. You're the man who seduced a young girl who didn't know any better and then killed her in cold blood. You destroy lives, Rufus Abernathy. You ruin families. You're a menace, a murder, and an aberration before God and the people of Charleston County. But the question you should be asking is who you're playing with. I'm the man who is going to put a stop to you. I'm the man who is going to expose you for the trash you are, and when it comes down to it, I'm the man who is going to slap cuffs on your ass and ensure that you spend the rest of your life in a dark, dank hole."

"You're a joke," Rufus said. "No one in this room will believe a word you say, and should you actually turn out to be stupid enough to try and accuse me, I'll turn it around on you." He shook his head. "You were Haley's boyfriend. You were the one who should have been with her the night she disappeared. Hell, half the people in this town think you're guilty anyway. I'll tell them you confessed the murder to me. I'll swear it on a stack of Bibles. Then we'll see who ends up in a hole."

Suddenly, the lights went low.

"What the hell is this?" Rufus asked.

"It's the truth, Professor Abernathy," Ryan answered. "You see, I knew Haley. I knew all of her hiding places, even if it took me awhile to remember some of them. Turns out a textbook wasn't the only memento of you she kept. Did you know Haley loved to record people, even when they didn't know she was doing so?"

Rufus's eyes went wide as a video of him kissing Haley started to play. You could hear the shock and disbelief run through the room like a tidal wave, one designed to destroy a man's reputation and finally bring justice to a twenty-year-old murder.

"Damn it," Rufus said.

As Ryan reached back to grab his cuffs, Rufus punched him in the face. He ran quickly, pushing a table over to block his path.

"No, you don't!" Ryan said and darted after the man.

While half the town sat around the opulent ballroom with their jaws scraping the floor, Ryan and his former professor ran out the doors, finding themselves standing face to face on the sandy Carolina shores.

"Give up," Ryan said. "It's over."

"You . . ." Rufus gritted his teeth. "You are nothing. You'll always be nothing."

"That may be," Ryan said, seeing the beach fill with a dozen other officers. "But I'm still better than you."

Chapter Thirty-Four

The warm South Carolina breeze glided across Ryan's face. The soft chirping of a blue jay carried through the cemetery, ricocheting from one headstone to another. He'd only visited Haley's grave a handful of times since her death, but after putting the man who'd ended her life behind bars, it only felt right to tell her in person.

The case was finally over and Haley's memory could finally be at rest. Ryan Devereux was no longer suspended, and the people of Charleston, South Carolina could finally mourn the young girl the way she deserved. Rufus Abernathy was behind bars with his reputation destroyed. It took twenty years, twelve stitches, and a world's worth of grief, but he'd managed to keep his promise.

"It's done." He knelt beside her grave even though he knew it was empty.

Ryan still remembered the day Haley's parents decided to hold a burial for their daughter three years after she disappeared. In the beginning, he was upset, questioning how they could have given up so soon without knowing for sure. It took years for him to understand the truth. The King family simply didn't know how else to deal with the grief and sadness tearing them apart. Perhaps they thought seeing her casket lower into the ground would help them deal with their emotions, that it would save the family. They were wrong.

Less than one year later, Haley's father was gone. After that, there wasn't much left of the Kings. Haley's one-time party throwing, cotillion-loving, proud Southern mother crumbled into nothing more than a recluse, spending her days walking the shores of her island home until finally leaving the Lowcountry for good.

"Rufus Abernathy is behind bars, right where he belongs." Ryan looked at the marble headstone near his feet. "I'm sorry it took so long." He took a deep breath, his eyes beginning to well up. "I finally got to see you in that dress though."

He spent the next few minutes just standing, listening to the world spin around him, listening to the air as it grew moist and dense with afternoon heat. He'd hoped maybe she'd speak to him. Maybe if he listened hard enough, he would hear her, but there was nothing, only the Carolina silence and his memories.

"Here you go," Chief Evans said as the sun began to melt into the crisp Atlantic waters. "Your badge."

"Thank you," Ryan replied, sliding it into his pocket.

"You were right after all." The chief smiled wide. "When I'm wrong, I say I'm wrong."

It wasn't at all necessary, but a few of his fellow officers had decided to throw a small beachside barbecue in honor of Ryan's work on the case, likely at the behest of his partner, though she'd never admit it. The smell of sweet, slow-roasted pork wafted across the sand, wrapping Ryan in a fragrant cloud. His stomach panged with hunger and his mouth began to water.

"You were right," Kit said, handing him an ice-cold drink. "You said you'd figure it out and you were right."

"What kind of cold-case detective would I be if I couldn't keep my promise?" he asked, watching the fading sun cast shadows across her sweet face.

"You're a damn good detective. Cold-case or any other."

In the distance, rising high out of the endless ocean, stood the Morris Island Lighthouse, the one he'd almost been driven into. The one intended to be an instrument of his death. Though he'd lived in Charleston his whole life, Ryan had never given much thought to the structure. He'd never really looked at it for longer than a few seconds.

Now that he had, though, he noticed just how weathered it looked, how tattered and worn with age. Looking at it, he couldn't help but see himself. That was just the way of things down here. Time changed you, the ocean, the heat, and the people. Each one had an impact on a man that was as inescapable as the Spanish moss, each one leaving its mark on you forever.

But most of all, it was the land itself, the feeling, the ambience, and the raw history of pride scattered over nearly every inch of his coastal home. It was that pride that was his driving force for all these years, and just like the lighthouse, he stood tall on that beach, having served his purpose and been proud to do so.

"What about later?" Ryan asked his partner, not sure what answer he was hoping for. "What are you doing later?"

"Me?" She gave a coy smile. "I'm not sure. But I know what you'll be doing."

"Really?" Ryan asked. "And what is that?"

Kit stepped closer, placing her hand on his chin. Squeezing it tightly, she slowly turned his head toward the coastline. "Her." He saw Michelle Myers standing at the edge of the sand. "Go on," Kit said. "She's waiting for you."

----------THE END---------

Click the image below to join my newsletter.

Or visit me at:

DavidBannerBooks.com

Made in the USA
Columbia, SC
06 January 2019